PRAISE FOR *ABBY SPENCER GOES TO BOLLYWOOD*

"Abby's extravagant travels and first romance are enough to satisfy and amuse."

—*Publishers Weekly*

"Readers will want for Abby what she wants for herself—to find her place in her two families—and should be touched and satisfied by the story's ending...this story showcases the glamour and grit of Mumbai, and gives readers an entertaining glimpse of backstage Bollywood."

—*Kirkus Reviews*

"There's some fun in Abby's first-class travel, budding romance, and dream-come-true scenario of one's unknown parent turning out to be a celebrity..."

—*Bulletin of the Center for Children's Books*

"Abby is a sweet, relatable character, but it's the lush backdrop that sets this book apart. The narrator describes the beauty and the extreme poverty of Mumbai."

—*School Library Journal*

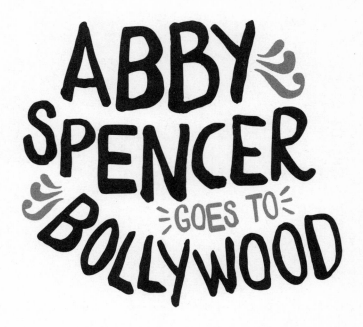

ABBY SPENCER GOES TO BOLLYWOOD

VARSHA BAJAJ

ALBERT WHITMAN & COMPANY
CHICAGO, ILLINOIS

꧁❦꧂

FOR JILL, WHO BELIEVED

꧁❦꧂

Library of Congress Cataloging-in-Publication Data is on file with the publisher.

Text copyright © 2014 by Varsha Bajaj
Hardcover edition published in 2014 by Albert Whitman & Company
Paperback edition published in 2015 by Albert Whitman & Company

ISBN 978-0-8075-6365-6

Printed in the United States of America.
10 9 8 7 6 5 4 3 2 1 LB 20 19 18 17 16 15 14

Cover design by Jordan Kost
Cover image © The Photo Commune/Digital Vision/Getty Images

For more information about Albert Whitman & Company,
visit our web site at www.albertwhitman.com.

ᘓ CHAPTER 1 ᘔ
BE CAREFUL WHAT
YOU WISH FOR

The one thing I want most in my life…? Hmm.

Miss Cooper needs to know that? Really?

My eyes dart from Zoey on my right to Priya diagonally across from me to the clock directly above Miss Cooper's head. Three minutes to the bell. Unlike me, my friends are scribbling furiously.

We're studying characters in literature and their deepest desires. I've read *Because of Winn-Dixie* every year since fifth grade. India Opal, my favorite character, wants to meet her mother. Miss Cooper said in her PBS voice, "Understanding your own desires will help you know the characters in novels better." When Miss Cooper orders and assigns, you do her bidding or go to detention.

I gnaw my pencil. Ever since I fell in love with the violin,

I've imagined a string quartet, the full enchilada—a cello, two violins, and a viola—providing a sound track to my life. I told Mom about it and she laughed. "Oh, Abby, you're funny! Most kids have an imaginary friend. You have a string quartet."

Mom gets me. It's always been Mom and me. We go together like the violin and the bow or apples and piecrust. We'd look like clones born twenty-one years apart except her hair is dirty blond and mine is as dark as the night. She says I have my dad's hair. He's Indian—as in, from India. And her lashes are a need-mascara length while mine are so thick and long, they look fake. But our brown eyes both turn lighter when the sun hits them.

As I reread and ponder the question, my string quartet picks up their bows and plays a deep, thoughtful song.

The bell buzzes.

I hurriedly scribble, *The one thing I want most in my life is excitement.*

Liar! My inner voice bursts out like an annoying pop-up on a computer screen and surprises me. *The thing you want most is to meet your father!* the inner voice accuses.

I strangle the voice. That is too personal. I could never whisper it, let alone write it down for a school assignment.

My life is a plate of perfectly edible but ordinary scrambled eggs. I want them savory, creamy, cheesy, and maybe with bacon on the side.

I don't want to seem ungrateful or anything. Life is okay, just too normal. Nice mom, adorable grandparents, decent school sprinkled with a few teachers I love and some I can't stand, and friends with *exciting* lives.

Zoey joins me as I throw things into my paisley-printed backpack. "Abby, you going to the Yogurt Cup with Priya and me?"

I nod.

Priya bounces over. "Race you to the bike stand!"

Juvenile, I think but race anyway.

We bike in silence down the winding suburban road lined with crape myrtle. Our bikes cut through the humid, still air as we make our way to the Yogurt Cup, our haunt during the summer. Frozen yogurt is our way of crushing the Houston heat that holds us hostage July through September and sometimes even longer.

The short ride has us sweating already, as if our bodies are screaming, *Need to cool down! Why are you outside? It's ninety-eight degrees! So what if it's early October and school's already started?*

When we reach the store, we lock up our bikes out front.

"Our exchange student from Norway arrives in six days," says Zoey. "Her name's Ingrid. She's a senior in high school."

Now *that* defines excitement. Why can't my family host an Ingrid from Norway?

"Should I have a party? Invite a bunch of people to welcome her?" Zoey knots her thick, straight hair.

"Yeah," says Priya. "It'll distract me from the fact that my sister's baby was due yesterday."

That also qualifies as excitement. Priya's older sister and her husband are expecting a baby.

Our bikes secured, we walk in and hug the cold air like a long-lost friend. The scent of peach blossomy cleaner greets us. The décor is candy colored and futuristic like a *Jetsons* cartoon, only cooler.

Besides the air-conditioning, Counter Guy is the other reason we love this place. Zoey has the biggest crush on him. Today she's wearing her favorite outfit, neon leggings and an oversized T-shirt with a swirly pattern, in case Counter Guy looks her way or telepathically guesses she wants to talk to him. He's a high school senior—grades out of Zoey's league, but so what?

When Priya once suggested that Zoey talk to him, Zoey almost fainted. Priya, on the other hand, is waiting for the day when Taylor Lautner gives up acting and enrolls in our school.

Me? I don't trust guys that much—other than my grandpa, of course. A smiling stork didn't drop me swaddled in a pink blanket with *Abby Tara Spencer* embroidered on it into Mom's arms from a puffy cloud. At thirteen, I know better. I have a father, but I've never met him.

Now, if my father suddenly burst into my life, *that* would be excitement. But that's as likely to happen as winter in July.

As I consider having a crush on a boy to introduce some thrills into my uneventful life, Zoey pokes me. "So, did I tell you guys that Ingrid from Norway plays the violin too, and she doesn't know much English?"

"She and Abby can speak through their music," Priya says in a Mrs. Cooper-PBS voice.

I reach for my favorite yogurt flavor, yellow cake mix. Mirroring her accent, I say, "My violin playing is as important to me as blood is to vampires."

Distracted, I fill too much yogurt in my cup, and it oozes onto my hand. At forty-two cents an ounce, yogurt puts a dent in a girl's money fast. I work hard for my yogurt money by helping at my mom's coffee shop, Slice of Muse. It's a coffee-for-your-zing, pie-for-your-tummy, and poetry-for-your-soul place.

"The two of you will bond through the purity of your vibratos." Zoey adopts the most pathetic excuse for an English accent.

I smack her with my pink plastic spoon. "We're doing Mrs. Cooper's voice, not Simon Cowell's!"

Yesterday I picked mango, strawberries—my fave fruit—and fruity pebbles. So today I choose different flavors. I pile on the toppings without really thinking. Chocolate chips, itty-bitty cheesecake things, and other stuff. If I'm going to pay for extra ounces of yogurt, I'm going to get my money's worth of toppings.

"It's not fair. You guys have all the excitement in your lives," I whine.

"You could have your name tattooed on your forehead or start playing your violin outside Target," suggests Zoey.

"Or I could dye my hair purple," I say, getting into the spirit.

"That will be three twenty-five," says Counter Guy, and Zoey turns red. You'd think he said, "You're cute. What are you doing Saturday evening?"

We pay and look over at our table. A group of kids has stolen it. Don't they know it belongs to the ZAP trio? Zoey, Abby, and Priya. In third grade, Zoey and I stood up for Priya when the popular girls called her mint-chutney-and-cheese sandwich moldy. Since then, we've been a team. Our team finds a different table.

Priya looks into my yogurt cup and says, "I read yogurt cups."

"Like tea leaves or tarot cards?" Zoey giggles.

"Yep." Priya looks serious.

I push my cup toward her. "Tell me my future, oh, all-seeing one."

Priya waves her spoon-wand and stares into my yogurt's soul.

"Are you a magician or a psychic?" I ask.

Priya shushes me. "I see you ruling the world one day…"

"While playing the violin," chimes in Zoey.

I grab my cup back and taste a spoonful of yogurt before it melts. Ice cold pleasure. The toppings all work together today. Some days they don't. Like when I got peanut butter morsels and strawberries.

Ooh, I taste something different. I dig around my cup to trace the new taste. Coconut flakes. I always thought I hated coconut—don't ask me why—so I've never chosen it before.

For a few minutes, we savor our yogurt in silence.

Then an itch on my cheek orders, *Hey! Scratch me.*

I put my spoon down and obey. My cheek feels hot. The itch takes possession of my forehead and arm.

Uh-oh. Frantic scratch, scratch, scratch.

Priya looks up from her yogurt, "Abby, your face! Did something bite you?"

Zoey tears her eyes away from Counter Guy. "Oh my God, you have big red splotches on your face!"

The itch mushrooms to my arms. I stare at my skin in the reflective tabletop. I look like a horrid picture of a diseased plant from a science textbook!

My lips are numb and the itch squeezes its fingers around my throat. I try to take a deep breath and can't.

What's happening?

Priya stands over me. "Oh my God, Abby. Your lips are huge."

"Like a cross between Angelina Jolie and Nemo," says Zoey, flailing her arms in the air.

I search for more air. I inhale the deepest breath possible but can't get enough. I inhale again and again. Am I hyperventilating?

Where has all the oxygen disappeared?

Seeing the panic in my eyes, Priya reaches for her cell phone. And can't find it. She grabs Zoey's. It has a low battery signal.

"Abby, are you dying?" Zoey shouts, panicked.

Counter Guy runs to our table with his cell phone in hand.

I itch, gasp, and try to feel my numb lips all at once. Priya grabs the cell phone and jabs 911. Zoey hops around and holds my hand.

"We need help at the Yogurt Cup on the corner of Chestnut and Rice," Priya orders. "My friend can't breathe. She's sick. Hurry!"

❧ CHAPTER 2 ❧
DNA

I gasp. Each breath is a struggle. The emergency medical people arrive within minutes of the 911 call.

They shoo everyone away from me, take my pulse, stare at my impression of a fish on a steel hook, radio the nearest ER, hoist me onto a stretcher, and head to the ambulance.

Priya and Zoey gather my stuff and scurry beside me.

All I want is a big gulp of oxygen and my mom. "Call Mom," I wheeze in Priya and Zoey's direction.

"We did already," says Priya. "And so did the EMT. She's on her way."

"We can't allow you to ride in the ambulance, but her mom is on her way," says the EMT. "Your friend is not alone."

"Don't worry, Abbs," says Zoey. "Text us the minute you get home."

The world around me swirls. The ambulance is like a dinosaur in the parking lot. People stare. I could die of embarrassment if whatever is happening to me doesn't kill me first. I should've worn my new crisp underwear, not the old comfy ones with faded pansies on my butt.

I'm only thirteen—too young to die. I haven't even had a boyfriend.

The doors to the ambulance close and we start to drive. I hear the EMT talking on the phone or radio or whatever. I hope God realizes nothing bad could happen to me; I need more time to trace my DNA.

If I die now, I'll have to come back as a creepy, frustrated ghost and haunt Mom. Like spirits with unfinished business do.

The EMT turns to me. I hear him through layers of sludge. Focus, Abby, focus.

"Are you allergic to anything?" he asks.

"I don't know."

Was that raspy, high-pitched voice mine?

When we hiked in the mountains in Colorado, I remember feeling like air was in short supply. This is a gazillion times worse.

A needle pierces my skin. A shot. Mercy of science. Medicine injected directly into my veins and I can breathe a little bit easier. But the red blotches on my skin still feel angry.

The ambulance stops and the doors open again. The EMTs wheel me into the ER. Mom arrives moments after us. She must have driven like Roadrunner with Coyote on her tail.

"Oh, honey! Oh, honey!" she chants. Her hair flies in all directions like the hay hair on our Halloween scarecrow. Her forehead is creased with worry, but her steps are determined. She's in Supermom mode, efficient and taking charge.

I take a breath and surprise myself. Abracadabra. Oxygen. I'm breathing normally. Was it the shot or having Mom with me?

They wheel me into a room and draw the green privacy curtain around us. Needles pinch me.

"We're putting in an IV and a heart monitor and checking your pulse and oxygen levels," the nurse explains. I have more wires and cords dangling from me than our computer at home.

The only shots I've had before this were immunizations when I was a kid. I'd clutch Mom's hand, squeeze my eyes tight, and turn my head sideways. After, we'd get ice cream on the way home to freeze out the memory of the stick. I'm not a kid anymore but we still got ice cream last year for old times' sake.

Here I am, with all these needles in my arm. It will take a lot of Rocky Road to freeze this memory!

Mom stares at the monitors. "Thank goodness, you can breathe. I called Grandpa and Grandma. They're coming too."

My grandparents, Mom's parents, live a street away from us. Even though we live in separate houses, our lives were one.

A dark-haired doctor walks in and introduces herself. "Abby, you scared a few people and yourself, today didn't you?" she says, patting my arm.

After checking me out and scanning my chart, she says, "You are both lucky. Abby had an allergic reaction and went into anaphylactic shock, but it wasn't full blown. Otherwise, we would've had to put in a breathing tube to help her breathe. Abby, did you eat or drink anything for the first time?"

I shake my head.

"Are you sure, honey?" Mom asks, massaging my hand.

"Did you take any medicine for the first time?" asks the doctor.

"No," I say.

Then I remember the heap of coconut flakes on my yogurt.

"Wait! Coconut flakes! I ate coconut flakes for the first time on my yogurt. Could that have done it?"

"You've never eaten coconut before?"

"I don't think so," I say, looking over at Mom. "Have I?"

"I remember you ate a bite of coconut cream pie when you were little. You hated it and spit it out."

"Are you allergic to it?" the doctor asks my mom. "Allergies can be hereditary. Not always though."

"No one in my family is allergic to coconut," says Mom.

"What about Abby's father?" the doctor asks.

Mom looks bewildered, as if she's never considered the other half of my DNA.

The words echo like in a movie. *What about Abby's father? What about Abby's father?*

What about my father? Is he allergic to coconut? My brain magnifies the questions and projects them onto a massive baseball stadium screen.

When my mom doesn't answer, the doctor says, "We'll keep you for a couple hours to monitor your vitals. We've also given you some Benadryl, so you'll feel drowsy. The red blotches will take a day or two to fade. I'm glad your breathing is back to normal. For now though, stay away from coconut in all forms, and, Abby, if you think of anything else you might have eaten, let us know. Mrs. Spencer, we will refer you to an allergist so you can pursue allergy testing."

As always, Mom lets the *Mrs. Spencer* fly.

"And the allergist will want to know Abby's father's medical history," the doctor says before patting me on the arm again and walking out.

Grandma and Grandpa Spencer rush into the room, their eyes shadowed with worry. When they hear I'm going to be fine, they sigh in relief.

I'm alive, and we exchange hugs and high fives. We'll celebrate when we get home.

For a brief moment, I'd imagined a full throttle violin concerto with me in first chair, wailing as the doctors diagnosed me with some horrible disease.

Wait a minute. Can I be the first chair and the patient? Whatever. That's what Benadryl does to your imagination.

I fumble through a text to Priya and Zoey. *I'm fine. Talk L8R. Did you remember my bike?*

As the Benadryl defeats me in the battle to stay awake, the doctor's question rings in my woozy mind. *What about my father? Does he have mile long sweeping lashes? Does he wonder if his daughter has his hair? Does he also hate coconut cream pie? Why has he never visited? Does he hate me?*

❧CHAPTER 3❧
EXCITEMENT IS EXHAUSTING

Mom and I drive home from the hospital in the vast, humid night. Can a question become so real that it can breathe? The one about my father rides home with us. My groggy mind clings to it like a Snuggie on a cold night—a little weird since it's so hot outside.

I'm still drowsy. I think my Benadryl shot was meant for the baby hippo at the Houston zoo. Also, it's two a.m. and a brush with death is exhausting. My imaginary string quartet snores.

But the ER visit and the doctor's reference to my dad have struck a nerve. My mind is racing with questions.

"How come my father never comes to visit me?" I ask Mom.

"Abby, are you unhappy?" she asks.

"No, I'm fine," I say. I'm not *unhappy*. Except I'd be happier if I knew my father. That's what I should have said.

"I want you to always be happy. Grandma, Grandpa, and I love you. We're family," she says, getting all gushy.

I'm happy and healthy and have a great family, even if it is different.

If my dad didn't care to visit me, why should I care about him?

Who needs a dad? It's his loss, not mine.

It isn't until later that I realize she didn't answer my question at all.

The next day, Mom wakes me up at noon. "I checked on you a million times last night. Didn't want to wake you too early this morning. You needed the sleep. Grandma is filling in for you at the café today. Grandpa wants to spend the day with you. Call him when you're ready. If you feel anything but 100 percent normal, *call me right away.*"

"Got it, Mom. I'm fine," I say and return her hug and kiss.

It's Saturday, the busiest day at Slice of Muse. Mom and her chef/business partner, Susan, will be knee-deep in latte and pie orders. Normally I'd be at the café helping and earning yogurt and jeans money.

I have a zillion texts from both Priya and Zoey since nine this morning. Maybe I can spend time with them and Grandpa.

When I call my grandpa, he picks up the phone on the first ring. "Good morning, Sparkles!"

Grandpa has always called me Sparkles. He claims my eyes glimmered when he first saw me—probably a minute after I was born. He's always been around, especially since my father hasn't.

I remember when I was in kindergarten, Grandpa came with me to Doughnuts with Dad Day at school. I chose chocolate-covered doughnuts for us and poured coffee for him and orange juice for me. Grandpa and I enjoyed every last crumb together.

"How come your grandpa came today?" Cassidy had asked after the first period bell rang and Grandpa left. "It's Donuts with *Dad*."

My red face matched my Elmo T-shirt.

Today I would have flipped back, "Dad, Granddad? What's the diff?"

But back then I was all soft-centered. The protective shell was not on the M&M yet.

"Families come in all shapes and sizes," I said, echoing the answer Mom gave whenever I asked her why my dad didn't live with us.

"I know that," said Miss Know-It-All. But one with a dad and a grandpa like mine is the best."

In that moment, my five-year-old self learned to bite back words. ("No, it's not! Mine is the best too.")

"I have a dad too. He just lives in India," I said.

"Does he ride on elephants?" she asked.

That afternoon at recess, I accidentally threw the basketball at Cassidy's head instead of the hoop.

At some point growing up, I learned to put on a poker face. *Relax all facial muscles, including the ones around your eyes,* I would remind myself when I was hurt by a comment about my missing father.

All of that feels so long ago as Grandpa and I make plans for a pool party with Priya and Zoey that morning.

Stomach rumbling, I go to the kitchen for a glass of milk. I smile at the sign Mom tacked to the fridge. On a sheet of yellow legal pad paper, she wrote in bold red marker, *Coconut-free zone—strictly enforced,* and pinned it with a magnet in the shape of a blueberry pie.

The doorbell rings, and Priya and Zoey fall all over me.

"We were so worried! We love you!"

We walk over to Grandpa's.

"Priya, remember how I thought our dads might be brothers when we were little?" I ask. After all, both our fathers are from India.

"Yes." Priya grins. "And we would imagine that we were long-lost cousins."

Mom met my dad, Kabir Kapur, in college and fell madly in love. Unfortunately, it didn't work out. After graduation, they broke up. My dad returned to India and never came back. Mom returned to Houston with a bachelor's degree in business. I was born eight months later.

We jump in the pool as soon as we get to Grandpa's place.

"Abby Tara Spencer, do you have sunscreen on?" Grandpa reminds me from the grill.

I clamber out of the pool. As I slop on the lotion, I remember when I tried to research my middle name. Tara— Hindi for *star*. Mom said my father often talked about his mother when they were dating, and Mom had taken an instant liking to her from the stories he told. My middle name was her nod to my father's mother.

Zoey sneaks up behind me and shoves me into the pool. All morning, we spray each other with squirt guns and play Marco Polo as if we're five. We race and make human towers and collapse into the forgiving water, giggling and sputtering.

Grandpa signals that lunch is ready.

Why do hotdogs taste better with friends and when you're trailing water from a soaked swimsuit?

After my friends leave, I flop on Grandpa's couch, and

we watch the baseball playoffs. Grandpa covers me with an afghan and strokes my hair.

Who needs a dad when you have a grandpa like mine?

Then I think about the note I wrote when I was six, asking my father to come visit. *Dad* in huge, tilted block letters filled the front of the envelope. I had written to Santa at Christmas and he had gotten my letter. I knew because I had asked for an American Girl doll, and he brought it for me. If Santa had gotten my letter, my dad would get my letter too.

Years later, I found the letter in Mom's memory box. It is an intricately engraved wooden box lined with velvet. Carved flowers and birds rise out of the wood. It also holds her brownie pin, the playbill from her junior high play, a BFF friendship bracelet, and a receipt from the post office.

Grandpa's voice brings me back from my time travels. "You okay, Sparkles? You've been awfully quiet."

"I'm fine," I say. "A little sleepy."

I doze off on the couch and dream that when I reached for the coconut flakes at Yogurt Cup, my dad emerged out of thin air, grabbed my hand, and said, "Abby, stop! You might be allergic to coconut like me."

⋤ CHAPTER 4 ⋥
TELLING TALES

I sense differentness the minute I walk into the house Monday, Mom's day off.

The house looks immaculate as if Mom has inherited Mary Poppins's skills. The floors gleam, tabletops and counters are visible, and the mounds of paper have disappeared to wherever clutter travels. Mom always cleans when she's stressed. A single rose in a one-stem vase on the dining table and an aroma of spices mimic a restaurant. Mom is cooking.

I find Mom in the kitchen. She gives me a hug. "I made the tandoori chicken that you love and rice pilaf and potatoes to go with it." I like to think that my half-Indian genes make me love tandoori spices.

She fidgets with her apron. Her eyes look like they're open too wide.

Whoa! This is the farewell dinner Mom made when she and her ex-boyfriend, Simon, parted ways. Is Mom planning to say farewell to me? Ha! Ha!

She and Simon dated for almost four years. They broke up when Simon got a new job that took him back to the Northeast, where his extended family lived. Mom decided she couldn't move. Her parents were here, she couldn't disrupt my life, and her business was taking off. The break-up was all civilized, kind of like an ad for Polo shirts. I was okay with them breaking up. I didn't want to move either.

"Wow! Is someone…coming over for dinner?" I ask suspiciously.

"No, no," Mom answers. "I thought we could have a nice evening. The two of us."

Distress signals go off—a symphony of alarm bells, church bells, and doorbells.

Mom pours herself a glass of red wine. She *never* drinks anything but water with dinner. This is too odd.

The string quartet plays the frantic "Flight of the Bumblebee."

"There's ten minutes before dinner. Do you want to shower?" Mom asks, all formal.

I dump my stuff and flee.

Zombies ate my mother and replaced her with whoever is downstairs.

I let the day's sweat wash away in the shower.

A thought enters my brain, like water trickling down the drain. *Am I going insane?* Why am I rhyming?

Are we going to have the Conversation? The one about my father. The one she said we would have when I'm *old enough?*

Could the allergy attack over the weekend and the doctor's questions about my medical history have made Mom realize it's time?

My sixth sense takes over my other five senses and my brain.

Then fear takes over. What if my father is an ax murderer or a pervert serving time in an Indian prison? And Mom hasn't told me to protect me?

Nah! Stop overreacting, I tell myself.

Maybe Mom's just relieved that I'm alive. Or maybe she hit a milestone at Slice of Muse.

I towel my hair dry and pull on my pj bottoms and T-shirt in a hurry to get downstairs.

Mom drains her glass of wine and serves the food.

"This looks awesome, Mom!"

"You remember I was trying to get the Epicure to carry our pies? I might be this close"—she gestures a pinch.

Pinprick to the balloon of hope.

"Oh wow! That's mega big," I lie.

"Yes. Keep your fingers crossed. We would triple our business if we succeed."

She pours me some cider in a wine glass and we toast. "To Slice of Muse taking over the world!" I manage to smile and say.

That's what all this is. Part of me is so disappointed it hurts. Part of me is weirdly relieved.

The string quartet in my head is confused. What music should it play? Sad, happy, disenchanted?

We eat. Mom has outdone herself. The chicken is tender and spiced perfectly. Peas and golden raisins make the rice yummalicious. "This is so good, Mom."

After putting the leftovers away, we move into the living room and sit on the couch with our buttermilk pies. A celebration dinner needed pie.

Without taking a bite, Mom puts her plate on the side table. She takes a swig of wine and blurts, "Abby, I need to talk to you about your father."

My stomach dives like a roller coaster.

I've waited and dreamed of this moment all my life. Now it's here. Hope waltzes with fear. I put my plate on the coffee table.

I gulp. I've practiced what I wanted to say for this conversation so many times. But where are the words when you need them? Instead, I stare at her blankly.

"My romance with Kabir had an expiration date, Abby," she says with a faraway look.

My heart squeezes painfully.

"You know we met while were both students in Dallas and that he is now in India," she continues and reaches for my hand.

"So he's not in prison?" I say, laughing in relief.

Her eyebrows rise. "Why would he be in prison?"

I can't stop laughing. "I was afraid that he might be a perv in prison and you were trying to protect me," I say between laughs.

She smooths her hair and looks a little confused. "He's far from a criminal, I know that about him."

What does she mean by that?

"Tell me more," I beg.

"Every little detail?" she tries to tease. But I can tell she's as nervous as I am and the joke is as flat as day-old Sprite.

She twirls a strand of hair and turns serious. "Abby, maybe I shouldn't have kept it a secret for so long. You have the right to be mad at me. I thought you'd understand better if you were older. I've been meaning to have this conversation for the past year and kept putting it off."

I don't say anything. Can you be thankful and angry

with a person at the same time? I feel both toward Mom right now.

"I always knew he'd return to India. Everyone who knew Kabir knew that about him. His big dream of becoming a news anchor in India consumed him. But he had a smile that could melt women. He had eyes that spoke and your ridiculously long lashes. His dreams and his drive made me forget reality. He was different, and I was in love."

I let her talk and soak in every word like a sponge. I touch my lashes—the ones like my father's.

"Our last meal together, the day before graduation, he made me apple pie and we laughed and cried and in a crazy moment he asked me to marry him."

I almost fall off my chair. "No!"

"But we both knew he didn't really mean it," she adds hurriedly. "I couldn't have left the country anyway. I couldn't imagine living in a different country, especially one with such a different culture. My life was here. Grandma was recovering from breast cancer. And we were young." She still has the distant look, as if she's looking through a window at her past.

"We were so young," she repeated, shaking her head. "He was twenty-two. I was twenty-one. We were babies."

The floodgate of questions gushes open. "Mom, why has

he never wanted to see me? Are you in touch with him? Where is he now? Why didn't he stay to see me?"

Mom refuses to look at me. She's almost peeled her nail off. I can see her gulp repeatedly. She looks as guilty as I had when I tried to hide a bad grade.

"Days after graduation, he returned to India. We never talked about the night he proposed. We talked a few more times after he returned home, but it wasn't the same. It was stilted, long distance, and awkward. The phone lines echoed back then. He had a new life and a new job and he was so excited. He had moved on…" he trails off.

"I didn't realize until later that I was pregnant. I tried to call after I found out. I spoke to Kabir's father, who didn't seem pleased to talk to me. I left messages. I waited by the phone. Kabir never called back. Finally, hurt and upset, I moved back to Houston to be close to my parents without giving him a new address or phone number."

I don't say a word. I feel cheated. How could she have given up so easily?

"Then I wrote him a letter, a very long one. I registered it, so I'd know that he got it. I still have the return receipt from the postal service. I told him about being pregnant…" Even after all these years, Mom's voice is strained.

The silence in the room speaks. Writing that letter must have been so hard.

Then she says softly, "Abby, he didn't call. He didn't write back."

The hole in my heart is as big as the Texas sky. I'm speechless. I've waited to hear this since forever. Had time stopped when Mom said those words? That's how it feels to me.

"How could it have worked anyway?" Mom asks the universe. "What would we have done even if he had answered?"

The world has stopped spinning. I know it did.

I pick up the plate of pie to give my hands something to do and then I look at it with revulsion.

"Mom," I ask. "What are you saying? Are you saying he doesn't care about me?"

She looks back at me, the truth in her shimmering eyes. "Abby, wait. There's more."

My father hadn't cared enough to call back. Holy Schmit! No wonder he had never come to visit me. Not because he was in prison or didn't have the money to travel. The jigsaw puzzle falls into place.

"You waited all these years to tell me this. I don't want to hear more. Really, I don't." I run to my room.

"Abby, wait. I knew you would be hurt. It's exactly why I waited to tell you. You were, and *are*, the most precious thing in my life."

He didn't care that I was walking around with his DNA. His dark hair. His ridiculously long lashes.

And his coconut allergy.

❧ CHAPTER 5 ❧
TWO–STEPPING
WITH ANGER

I wake up battered by dreams, but I can't remember them. This is my first day knowing that my dad didn't care enough to even contact my mom when she wrote him that she was pregnant.

Why has nothing changed? Shouldn't the sun at least not shine so bright?

I brush my teeth as if I'm trying to strip the enamel. Like brushing hard is going to erode my anger. Can I crawl back into bed and lie there wallowing in anger mixed with letdown? Anger + letdown = anglet or angdown…whatever.

I rummage through my laundry basket for a pair of not-too dirty jeans. I find a pair and scramble into them. As I pull on my orchestra T-shirt, I remember the director telling us we'd get a new piece of music today. In spite of my messed-up life, I feel the anticipation. Maybe the music would be as dramatic as my turmoil.

Pots and pans clang in the kitchen. What is Mom doing this early?

The aroma of blueberry pancakes lures me downstairs. Weird! That's a weekend breakfast. Did I sleep through the week?

There it is. A stack of pancakes with a slather of butter between each one, the way I like them. That way the butter melts into each pancake. Mrs. Butterworth stands with her hands together.

Mom hovers, eager to satisfy my every need instead of sipping her coffee and watching the *Today* show like normal. What do you want to drink? Orange juice or milk?

Really?

I want to dig into the stack to fill the hole in my life. Maybe the syrup will soak up the anglet feeling.

But I don't. The string quartet plays an angry concerto.

Bonding over pancakes was what we did on weekends growing up. She would top them with chocolate chips, blueberries, raspberries, or Craisins. The choice of topping depended on our mood. When I was little, she used molds to make hearts and bears. She'd taught me to look for the bubbles before I flipped them so they would be perfect. A few years ago, we retired the molds. Who knew—pancakes taste just as good round.

Sharing pancakes that morning would seem wrong. Last night I was told that my father didn't bother to reply when he found out about me. My anger has been building since yesterday. Seriously, Mom? Does she think pancakes can fix how I feel?

How would my life have been different if my father had been thrilled to hear I was coming into this world? Would he have eaten pancakes with us? Would he have loved me?

"I'm not hungry," I say.

"Abby, have a bite. A little one."

Oh, I want to.

"I'm not hungry," I snap. My voice is flinty. It has to be if I have to get those words out. I realize I'm getting angry with the wrong person. Mom had me, by herself. After all, she has been the one to raise me. She was around and my dad wasn't. I should be mad at him, but he isn't here to be mad at.

Mom blinks several times as she picks up the untouched plate of pancakes and puts it aside.

"Should I tell Priya and Zoey that my dad doesn't care about me?" My laugh is hollow.

"You can do whatever you want," she says, resigned, as she slides the pancakes down the garbage disposal and hits the grind switch. The whirring metallic noise makes me wince.

"Abby, we have to talk about Kabir—I mean, your father," she says as she yanks the dishwasher open and almost throws the plate in. She grips the counter and takes a deep breath. "I plan to reach out again and try to find him. Contact him and find out his medical history. I waited this long because I knew all this would be hurtful. But really, there is more I need to tell you."

"Bit late don't you think? Do they make Hallmark cards for the occasion? Where do you find them? Are they under *Surprise, your daughter is a teenager?*"

Listen to yourself, Abby. You sound like a witch. But I can't help it.

Mom makes a peace offering. She reaches for my arm. "I'll dig through my stuff and find his contact information. Abby, we were young. Too young and we made mistakes. I am sorry."

My hands shake as I get onto the school bus. I'm that big fat mistake they made and I have to be forgive them for being too young?

My discovery for the day: two-stepping with anger introduced me to my dark side. Who knew you could stumble into the shadows without being bitten by a vampire or doing drugs?

Maybe discovering my dark side will bring another layer to my violin playing like famous violinists with tragic lives.

Abby Spencer, violinist. Her dark side meets the bow and the strings vibrate to produce the next violin prodigy.

Priya and Zoey are already at the lockers getting stuff together when I get to school. "Hey," I say as I jiggle my locker open.

Part of me wants to blurt out: *You guys, I know now that my father didn't even reply to my mom when she told him she was pregnant. Ha! Funny, huh?*

But I need more time to figure things out. Find answers to the questions they might ask if I start that conversation.

Questions.

I have questions I haven't asked yet. Last night my brain floundered and struggled to keep afloat. Did my father fulfill his dream and become a newscaster? If he had stayed in America, would their romance have had an expiration date? If he had reacted differently, would she have changed her life plans? Is he married? Does he have other children?

Priya has her arms loaded with her algebra textbook, binder, and homework folder. "You look pale. Are you okay?"

My stomach rumbles. Loud. Oh great. I figured people with tortured souls didn't need breakfast.

"I didn't eat breakfast and obviously I need food," I say, embarrassed.

Zoey fishes out a beaten, crumpled granola bar from the depths of her locker. "Want this?"

"Eeew." Priya wrinkles her nose.

A prehistoric granola bar from the depths of a locker is my punishment for turning down a loving blueberry apology on a plate.

My stomach couldn't rumble and attract attention in algebra. I shrug and take the bar. A girl has to do what a girl has to do.

"Anyway, Abby," said Priya. "I have a big favor to ask. You know how there's International Day tomorrow? Mom's doing a booth on India and she wants me to dress in Indian clothes, but I really don't want to." Priya takes a deep breath, and her eyes beg.

"Why not?" I ask, puzzled.

"I don't want to be gawked at."

Priya does hate speaking in public. I guess this falls in the same category.

"Wait, are the clothes ugly?" interrupts Zoey.

"Nooo!" says Priya. "I wouldn't make a great model. Abby would be so much better, right? Zoey, I'd ask you except you're a foot taller, and none of my clothes would fit you. Abby, will you do it? Mom wanted me to ask you for days and I didn't and she's mad."

"Do I have to twirl around?" I grin. "I'll do it!"

Hey, I'm the perfect choice. I'm half-Indian after all, even if I look part Caucasian. A chance to try on my identity!

Priya sighs with relief. "Thanks, Abby. You'll do a great job. You're such a performer. I'm a behind-the-scenes person."

How ironic! I'd be wearing Indian clothes. I'm a performer. Like my dad, the newscaster. Maybe I inherited more than his hair and lashes. Is my DNA calling?

❧ CHAPTER 6 ❧
SERIOUSLY?

Mom sits on the living room floor (crisscross, applesauce) with a million pictures scattered around her and a couple of empty shoeboxes. She scans and searches her past. I always wondered why she didn't have a picture of my father in a picture frame or at least in a keepsake box.

Now I understand. She must have been so hurt at his indifference. I would have been hopping mad. Typically, Mom is not the angry type. She thinks anger is a waste of energy.

"Hi, Abby! How was your day?" she asks. Mom tries hard to be normal-upbeat but I think I see her try to wipe a tear away without me noticing.

The question hangs in the air.

"I should've had your dad's picture more available, but I didn't. It was too painful."

Typical Mom. I would have probably ripped his pictures if I were in her shoes.

I grab a bag of Chex Mix and go to my room exhausted. She gave me one of my dad's pictures a long time ago—a head shot, like a driver's license picture but slightly bigger.

In an alternate reality, I might have grown up bilingual with two parents. Instead of coping with living without a father, I might have had to cope with living between two cultures. Pick your issue, Abby. I know my father like I'd know a missing tooth that my tongue wanted to feel. He's a gap.

I must have nodded off after eating my snack because Mom yelling my name pierces through my sleep. "Abby, Abby! I found more of Kabir's pictures."

I rub my eyes, will them open, and stumble downstairs. She stands at the bottom of the stairs clutching a four-by-six piece of my identity.

I'm afraid to look. Gingerly, I take the pictures from her hand.

Okay, confession time.

Since I'd only seen that one stilted yearbook/driver's license picture of my father, I've filled that vacuum by knowingly creating a picture in my mind. It is a cross between Grandpa, Priya's dad, and the dad in the movie *Cheaper by the Dozen*.

I chose Grandpa, because—duh—he is the closest

thing to a father figure I've ever known. I chose Priya's dad because he's sweet and kind and the only Indian man I know well. *Cheaper by the Dozen* was my favorite movie when I was a kid. I watched it on every long car trip. Being an only child, I yearned for the chaos of a big family, and the dad in it is hilarious.

Some websites mash up two celebrities' faces and the computer generates an absurd image of how their baby would look—like Miss Piggy and Justin Bieber.

I therefore imagined my own mash-up of my father. A man with Grandpa's pudgy belly and love handles, *Cheaper by the Dozen* dad's prominent Adam's apple, Priya's dad's jet-black hair that's so like mine. My imaginary father would also take vitamins like Mom and like to fix dripping faucets and clogged garbage disposals like Grandpa. He would like '80s rock and be a math whiz like Priya's dad and he would yelp a lot and be all gangly and double-jointed like the *Cheaper by the Dozen* dad.

Now as I stare at the real picture in my hand, the reality of my father challenges me. I have to replace the imaginary father I've lived with for all these years with the real thing. I wish there is a *Find and Replace All* command for real life like on my computer.

The images of the real man smiling at me knock me on my butt.

Even though this picture is old and he has weird hair and a mustache. My. Father. Is. A. Hottie. LOL. Ugh! Ugh!

He's my dad. He's not supposed to be hot.

He wears jeans and a scruffy T-shirt. His eyes say *I'm good looking and I know it.* I can tell he's about as tall as Grandpa—maybe five feet, ten inches, or so, his hair is thick and wavy. He has bony wrists, a square jaw, and my twinkle in his eye. With bare feet and jeans rolled up, he holds what looks like a miniscule minnow on a fishing rod. He goofs around, pretending he's caught the hugest whale ever.

Mom stands behind me and for a moment, I forget to be angry and lean back into her. Even though I don't trust boys and have never had a boyfriend, in my gut I understand why she might have fallen for him.

"Ew, what's with the mustache?" I say. Like it matters.

"Kabir said all the guys in India grew mustaches." Mom humors me.

In the second photo, my mom and dad gaze into each other's eyes pathetically. Mom's hair is much longer and more layered than now. She's skinny like me and drooly.

Now that the box is opened, I wanted to dig into its depths. I want to make up for the years when I didn't know my dad. I want to replace the fictional father in my head with reality. Even if he doesn't care about me and, therefore, I shouldn't care about him.

Mom and I wordlessly go through the stack of pictures from her college days. There are a few more with my dad in them. There are pictures of them at college events, graduation, with a group of friends, and one of my dad at the Houston Intercontinental Airport.

"I took that when I drove him to the airport that last time fourteen years ago. I didn't know I was pregnant yet," she whispers.

I don't have a smart comeback. The drums are not beating. The dance with anger is over for this moment. "Can I have these?" I ask.

She nods. "Abby, I should've shown you all the pictures, but the memories were so painful. The Kabir I fell in love with was so kind and considerate. Not at all like the person I tried to contact when I realized I was pregnant. I couldn't imagine him ignoring my calls and letters. But he did and..."

"Mom, let's talk more later, okay?" I hurry to my room and spend the next hour staring at each picture as if I want to memorize them, brand them onto my brain. A part of me is disgusted with him. Still he's my father and I want to know him.

Later that evening, we walk over to my grandparents' for dinner. They know that Mom and I talked about my father.

The silent, meaningful looks exchanged between them and Mom tell me the story.

The story I want to hear is what do they think of it? How did they feel when my father didn't respond to Mom's calls and letters? Were they upset?

But I don't go there. We eat dinner like awkward strangers. Everyone is extra polite to each other. I can imagine them all deciding, "Let's not bring it up till after dinner."

I pick at my salad and play with my spaghetti. After mutilating the noodles, I excuse myself, saying I have a lot of homework.

"Abby, we thought we would all sit down and talk," Mom says.

Now they want to talk. Well, I don't.

"Not tonight. I have homework."

On my walk home, I imagine them all agreeing that I need time. I make a beeline for the computer and google Kabir Kapur. I googled him once a few years ago. A couple images came up that didn't match the picture I had and I heard Mom enter the room so I slammed the computer shut and gave up. I didn't want to upset Mom. And he didn't ever visit or try to contact me, so why should I try to find him? Now I'm ready.

Two Kabir Kapurs pop up. One is a bald doctor who lives in Seattle. Another sells furniture in Dubai.

Dead end.

I try a new search.

I type *Kabir Kapur TV anchor India* and hit Enter.

Zero, zilch, nada. Poor Dad. I guess he didn't achieve his dream of becoming a news anchor. Serves him right for leaving Mom and me.

I stare at the monitor vacantly. Then my eyes register an entry for Wikipedia at the bottom of the page.

The first line reads *Kabir Kapur is the birth name for Naveen Kumar, a Bollywood film star.*

What's Bollywood? It rhymes with Hollywood. Don't Priya's parents watch Bollywood movies?

For kicks or because of some urge I can't explain or my sixth sense, I google Naveen Kumar—6,992,831 hits.

As Grandpa would say, holy guacamole! Or oh Schmit!

Bollywood actor! Bollywood star! Bollywood box-office sensation! Bollywood heartthrob!

My heart starts to skip beats. I click to enlarge an image of Naveen Kumar.

OMG.

It. Is. My. Father.

He looks older and glossier than in the picture Mom showed me. But it's him. Unmistakably him. Laughing at me from the screen. His eyes crinkle like in the picture with Mom.

And why isn't he wearing a shirt in some of these pictures? Bollywood sex symbol? I thrust my chair away from the desk. This is so wrong and so unfair. The string quartet has put down their instruments and they are staring too.

The mouse clatters to the floor. I step away from the computer as if it's about to explode and I need to evacuate.

I call Mom at my grandparents' house. "Mom, you and Grandma and Grandpa have to come here *now*!"

As I wait for them, I look at the images again. I can't stop. Does Mom know this? Or was she too hurt to google his name? Or is this the "more" that she mentioned?

↪ CHAPTER 7 ↩
MY DAD'S A STAR!

Mom, Grandma, Grandpa, and I huddle around the computer in our little study. Our eyes wide, we stare at the ultimate fan site for Naveen Kumar. It's as if we've been told the world is no longer round.

Mom looks pale. "Do I know this Naveen?" Mom mutters.

This guy is supposedly a Bollywood legend. Is he the same guy who went to college with Mom and wanted to be a TV anchor?

"Mom, why didn't you ever google my dad in all these years?" I blurt.

"I did, Abby. But it was years before I tried searching. At first, the hurt and rejection felt like shackles that I could never break free."

What? I'm not sure I get it, but the words make me pause and look at Mom differently.

I'm too overwhelmed to utter a word.

"Then, as the years passed, the hurt was not as raw, and I googled him. I discovered Naveen Kumar. I told you I had more to share," Mom says, pacing the room.

"I realized he didn't seem to want any part of his time in Dallas. He had moved on. I was scared that he might think I was a stalker or wanted part of his fame or money. And I had to think about how his fame would affect you. I wanted you to have a normal life. The last year or so as you got older, I was scared you would search and find him." Mom looks at me, hoping for understanding, I think.

I don't know what to say.

Mom takes a deep breath and continues. "I read how his life was an open book and how he was always followed by the media. The media speculated about his romances, when he would marry, and why he wasn't married. I knew I owed you more information, but honestly, Abby, the idea of a life without privacy makes me shudder." Mom's voice is shaky and her face is drained of color.

Grandma and Grandpa have heard this before. I can tell by the looks on their faces. Grandma retreats to the kitchen to make chamomile tea and to give us privacy. Chamomile tea would be her answer if a hurricane rocked the house, which is what this feels like.

"I'll be darned!" says Grandpa, trying to lighten the air in the room. "Holy guacamole! Sparkles, your father is a Bollywood sex sym—" he stops and corrects himself, seeing the horrified look on my face. "A Bollywood film star!"

Sex symbol! The word that rhymes with Tex-Mex made the assembly last year giggle in embarrassment. And it was only mentioned in the lyrics of a song. Of course, it was mainly the sixth graders who snickered and shuffled.

In the world according to Abby, sex anything should not be used to describe my father.

Then my grandpa gets serious. "Abby, we all felt that you should have a life away from celebrity till you were older. Your mom planned to tell you soon."

In a weird way, Grandma's chamomile tea actually works and calms us a bit. Maybe it's the familiar thing when everything else is upturned and blown away.

After my shock wears off, Mom decides to thoroughly search the Internet. The old phone number she has isn't even valid anymore. With 6,992,831 hits, she thinks one might lead us to a way to contact him. But it's like looking for a needle in the Internet haystack. Fan sites and gossip sites clutter everything.

After hours of searching and not finding anything, I'm

exhausted. It's after ten. My mind hurtles between a rock and a mound of homework.

I want to meet him. But I don't want to meet him.

Mom should've told me. Maybe she shouldn't have.

Maybe I should find a daisy and strip its petals to find my answer. Instead, I gnaw at my nails. Finally, my grandparents leave and I go to bed. I leave Mom still hunched over the computer, mesmerized.

The next morning, I still have to go to school. It's International Day, and I promised Priya I'd model Indian clothes. Mom has bags under her eyes the size of puffy caterpillars. She bravely chugs coffee at the kitchen table, trying to wake herself. Without looking up, she says, "I told Susan about all this and she's been incredibly supportive. I'm running late again. But I was up till three. I found a web site for a production company that your father seems involved in and it had a contact number. With daylight saving time, there's a ten and half hour time difference. I checked. I plan to call tonight."

"What will you say when you call, Mom? Please let Naveen-Kabir know he has a thirteen-year-old American daughter?" It's so absurd I start to giggle.

Mom spits out her coffee and cracks a smile. "Welcome back, Abby's sense of humor, even if it is snarky. Have a great time at International Day. We'll figure it out, honey," she says and I leave for school.

What exactly would we figure out? What to say? How to get a hold of my father? Or where do we go from here? I'm so preoccupied that I could have eaten a spatula instead of my toaster waffle and not known it. I stare out the window on the ride to school instead of chatting as I did most mornings.

When I get to school, I head toward the gym in a daze. As soon as I walk into the gym, I say aloud, "Wow!"

An array of flags has transformed the All-American gym into a United Nations assembly hall. There are at least twenty-five festive booths representing different countries. Volunteer moms bustle around getting their tables ready.

The air is soaked with the aromas of food. Butter croissants from France, bite-size tacos from Mexico, Greek spanakopitas, Indian samosas, and custard tarts from England.

I stand at the entrance for a minute and take it all in, feeling excited. I head toward Priya's booth, where Zoey is waiting. Priya's mom has draped our table in a cloth embroidered with mirrors and arranged a few artifacts from India on it. Currency, jewelry, books, fabrics, and an intricately carved rosewood box. It looks like the one Mom has at home with her memory stuff. I wonder if my father gave that to her. A huge map and posters swirl around the table.

The new knowledge about my dad gives the objects

new meaning. It feels right that I'm volunteering at the India booth. But what do I know about India even if my father is there?

It's in South Asia.

Priya's parents came from there.

I love samosas and chicken tikka.

Oh! And Gandhi was Indian.

Wow. It smacks me in the face. I don't know much! I have so much to learn.

Mrs. Gupta is setting up her laptop with the help of the tech guy when I walked up to her. "Hi, Abby, we're almost ready," she says. "Here are your clothes. Priya will help you get dressed." She reaches out to hold my hand. "And Abby, thank you so much for doing this."

"You're welcome. Why do you have the laptop, Mrs. G.?" I ask, peeking into my bag of clothes.

"Oh, I have a music video that I'd like to show if we can get it working," she replies.

Priya and I rush to the locker rooms. I open the bag to find the dressiest, most ornate, and stunning outfit I've ever seen. The skirt is pale bluish-purplish silk. Gold and silver embroidery adorn the hem. The blouse is pink, trimmed with the same lavender color from the skirt.

"Wow! Priya, this is gorgeous. What if I ruin it?" I slip into the skirt and blouse.

"You won't ruin it," Priya says as she buttons me up. She pleats the scarf, which matches the skirt, and drapes it around the skirt, partially covering the sliver of exposed midriff between the skirt and the blouse. She throws the other end of the scarf over my shoulder.

And voila! I'm ready. It looks like a sari, but it isn't. A sari, Priya tells me, is six yards of untailored fabric draped around the body.

I looked in the mirror admiring myself and then it strikes me. This isn't just International Day. It's a debutante ball for Abby Tara Spencer.

Overwhelmed by the discovery that has catapulted my life to crazyville in the last twenty-four hours, I grab Priya's hand. She looks at me and then at her watch. "You look amazing, Abby. We better get back to the gym before Mom comes looking for us."

In a saner frame of mind I would've realized this isn't a Kodak moment. But my mind is whirling. I grab Priya's hand tighter and whisper urgently, "Priya, what if I told you I learned a lot more about my father?"

"Abby, not funny." Priya packs my clothes. "We need to get back before the bell rings."

I can't blame Priya. She doesn't know my life has taken a mega twist. No normal person chooses to make major life-changing announcements in the locker room. *Not* with the sounds of metal locker doors clanging. *Not* with the faint smell of sweaty socks from a million years wafting around. *Not* with minutes left to the bell.

Sure enough, the bell buzzes like a chain saw.

"And what if I told you my father is very famous in India?" I whisper as Priya opens the locker room door and we're thrown upstream into a sea of kids heading to class. I guess once I start, I can't stop, even if Priya thinks I'm being funny.

Priya gives me a look that says, *Ha! Ha! Hilarious.*

We run back to the gym and take our places at the booth. Priya looks at me and says, "What's up with you? As far as I know wearing that outfit doesn't make you a fantasy writer."

I can't answer because volunteer moms oohing and aahing over my outfit have surrounded me.

Mrs. Gupta has her laptop working. Kids file into the gym, their pretend passports in hand. They go from table to table, picking up information, food samples, and stamping their passports with visas from each country's booth.

Then they're at our table. Mrs. Gupta does her mandated spiel laced with facts. India is the world's largest democracy, it's a secular country, Hindi is the national language, etcetera.

Learn, Abby. Slow down, Mrs. G.

Then it's time for me to twirl as she explains that a girl would wear this dress on a special occasion like a wedding. I strut and twirl to let the students see and admire the beautiful fabric. Priya claps the loudest. Mrs. Gupta thanks me and announces, "To end, I'd like to show you a song and dance clip from a Bollywood movie. It's like the music videos we have on MTV."

She points the remote and a pulsing beat of exuberant music fills the gym. In the video, girls in outfits like mine dance in sync to the beat of the music. It's beautiful and mesmerizing. The infectious rhythm has me tapping my feet even if I don't understand the lyrics. And then my father—yes, my father—erupts onto the screen and winks at the camera.

I freeze.

Mrs. Gupta presses a button on the remote and pauses my father in mid-leap. "That's India's biggest star, Naveen Kumar. You could compare him to Brad Pitt."

I expect him to spring out of the computer monitor and into the gym. I feel like my stomach could jump out of my body at any moment. She unpauses my dad and he finishes his leap and launches into a dance routine designed to get people on the floor and moving…unless you happen to be his mortified, unknown-to-him daughter. Kids clap to the beat, moving their hips. It's infectious. Even the principal taps his foot.

But not his daughter and her embarrassed friend Priya,

who whispers, "I told Mom not to play that. It's so corny and Naveen Kumar is a doofus. No idea why the females of the world swoon over him."

Priya has covered her face with her hands. She peeks at the screen through her fingers.

Zoey disagrees. "You're kidding, right? He's super cute. Look at his moves."

I want the earth to open up and swallow me. I'm not sure which is worse. Priya's disdain or Zoey's crush.

Yet my father-famished eyes study the image, soaking up syllables in a language I don't understand. Trying to absorb and memorize every nod, squint, and movement.

"He's someone's dad, Zoey!" I say before I can grab the words back.

"He's not married," chimes in Priya.

"Maybe he has a love child," I say.

Why is a child born out of marriage called a love child? Why is the child not called an oops? Once upon a time, the love child was called ugly names like bastard. My skin crawls in protest.

"You're talking crazy today. What's gotten into you?" Priya asks.

I force out a crazy laugh and make googly eyes. They both join in.

Zoey does the Naveen Kumar dance moves.

And then I swallow, looking Priya in the eye and just blurt it out, "Naveen Kumar is my father."

Zoey says, "Sure, and there will be world peace in 2015."

"You guys, I am serious," I whisper urgently.

Priya looks at me like I'm speaking Mandarin or Portuguese or a combination of the two. Then she rubs her eyes as if I've grown two heads.

Zoey realizes I'm serious. Her mouth hangs open. If a fly wanted to visit her stomach, it could've had a direct flight.

Priya keeps staring and then goes red and stammers, "I didn't mean what I said about Naveen Kumar being a doofus."

"It's okay, Priya. You didn't know."

"You made fun of her dad! You did, you did!" Zoey sings. "I am now the bestest friend, you are not."

"Naveen Kumar is your dad? OMG, Abby!" Priya shrieks.

"You guys, keep it to yourselves for now. I need to figure things out first. My mom is trying to reach him. And I just don't know how this will all go down."

I don't tell them that he didn't care about me and didn't contact my mother when she wrote him. That thought shrivels my heart. The words could never escape my lips.

He may be a big star but he is a lousy father.

❧ CHAPTER 8 ❧
STAR-CROSSED

On the ride home after International Day, I chew my lip. How would Mom call Naveen Kumar, a famous Bollywood star, and ask him for his medical history? Especially since he has so totally disowned his past and moved on.

I wouldn't want to be in her shoes.

She keeps her word and calls the production company that night. Grandma offers to come over and hold her hand, but Mom declines. She even shoos me away. I try to pretend it's a normal evening like any other. Ha! I go to the next room and try to eavesdrop through the closed door but Mom has the TV on so I can't hear.

Five minutes later Mom shrieks, "Abby! Abby!"

I race out, my heart pumping. Is my father on the phone? Not quite. But we're getting closer.

Mom speaks with a secretary at the production company who confirms that Naveen Kumar is indeed Kabir Kapur. Like we don't know that by now. She refuses to give Mom his contact number, even after she explains that she knew him in college but lost touch with him. Mom says the woman's cynical and exhausted tone suggests she's heard similar stories before.

Mom leaves her contact number and a message for Kabir/ Naveen/Dad. *I need to get in touch with you. It's important.* Not *Your teenage daughter who you don't care about almost died of a coconut allergy. Do you have one too?*

Morning. Afternoon. Evening. A whole day passes. No phone call.

Mom's discreet message is obviously easy to ignore, or maybe the lady threw it in the trash. A week later, Mom calls again and begs the woman to relay her message to my dad. Mom thinks the woman takes her message more seriously the second time.

Monday. Tuesday. Another eternal week. No phone call. Each time the phone rings we jump. We go through the motions waiting for life to take off. I forget to study exponents and my grade in algebra drops exponentially.

"Mom, have you checked your email today?"

We both know why I ask.

"And how would he get my email address?" she snaps.

All this waiting and hoping is making me nauseated. I decide I don't need a father who doesn't wear a shirt anyway. A father who is a Tex-Mex symbol is so unnecessary to a happy life.

Priya and Zoey ask about the dad situation and I snap, "I don't want to talk about it—ever."

Being good friends, they back off. "If you change your mind, we're here," they offer.

Mom calls a third time. Her voice quivers as she begs and cajoles the woman. Part of me wants to snatch the phone away and say, "Enough!"

The day after the third call, Mom and I are watching *Chopped* on the Food Network when the phone rings. I snatch it on the first ring.

"Can I speak to Meredith Spencer, please?" a stranger asks.

"May I ask who's calling?" I say even though my sixth sense knows. His accent is different—a lot like Priya's parents' accents, but not like Apu's on *The Simpsons*. A little singsong.

"Naveen."

I mutely throw the phone to Mom like it's cootie covered. Silently I mouth, "My father."

Mom takes the phone. Her face is drained of color as she walks to her bedroom. The air around me goes still and I watch TV as if it's in a foreign language. My mind races. Will he want proof from Mom? Will he want a DNA test like in those horrible TV talk shows?

I sit motionless and stare at the old-fashioned clock on the wall. Tick. Tick. Tick. It has never ticked so loudly or so slowly or so ominously.

An eternity later, Mom emerges from the bedroom. Her eyes are red.

"I told him." She combs her shaky fingers through her hair. She looks me in the eye and repeats, "I told him," as if she couldn't believe she's actually done it.

"And what did he say?" I ask in a strangled voice.

"He was stunned and angry. Abby, he says he never got my letter or messages. I told him I talked to his dad. Naveen said he had moved to Delhi for a job. We talked about that for a while. We're both confused." Mom shakes her head in disbelief. "Someone *must* have gotten my letter," she whispers to herself. "I got the receipt that the letter was received."

Time stands still in a haze of confusion.

I thought of many possibilities but not this one. Never this one.

I feel like my spine has suddenly gone limp.

What does this mean?

"He just didn't know?" I ask. "He didn't know I existed?"

So he *didn't* not care. He didn't disown me. He didn't mean to move on and leave Mom and me in the dust.

Mom nods. She's as pale as a polar bear. Her eyes glisten with tears. "He doesn't understand why his father would not have told him that I called. His father died a year after you were born, so I guess we'll never know. He asked a lot of questions about you. Do you look like him? What are you like? He wants me to email your picture."

I'm quiet, absorbing every word. Movies that portray earth-shattering emotional moments with a lot of screaming and shrieking couldn't be further from the truth. The truth is quiet and bewildered.

Mom gets quiet too. She sits down on the couch and turns toward the TV. I don't think she's watching it so much as staring through it.

I stare out at the oak tree in the yard. I haven't noticed the bird nest in the tree before.

An hour passes or maybe two.

I try to practice my violin. But each time I play, it scratches and whines. Why did I ever take up the violin? It's too difficult.

An hour later, the phone jangles. This time I don't leap on it. Mom answers. I hear her say, "Kabir, I was hurt, angry, betrayed. I thought you didn't care that I was having your baby," before she steps out of the house and into the backyard.

Oh, what a mess. Or as Miss Cooper would say in her PBS voice, "What a tangled web we weave."

I pick up my violin again and this time there is no scratching or whining. The notes come out just right and I understand why I love it. I pour my anguish into my bow, and the sound reflects my feelings.

Mom comes in, her shoulders drooped. "He wants a couple of days to digest all this. I told him that I found out he's a movie star a few years ago but decided to not tell you because I wanted you to have a normal childhood. *That* he understood but was still upset." Mom's voice breaks.

"Mom, is he married? Does he have other children? Do I have half-brothers or sisters?" All my questions spew out at once.

"No, Abby, he is not married and does not have children."

I'm not sure why, but I'm relieved to hear that.

Mom speaks again. "His mother—your grandmother—is very sick. She's in the hospital. He's overwhelmed to begin with and then this is all too much. He wants to ask her if she knows anything about the letter I wrote, but this isn't the time."

Mom gets up and gives me an awkward hug. Someday I'll ask her what it felt like to talk to him after all those years. "Abby, he does have an allergy to coconut."

A tear rolls down my cheek without my permission. Somehow, that little coconut tidbit connects us as I try to make sense of my crazy world.

The next morning, as I rush to get to school, the phone rings. I don't pick up. I'm scared.

"Abby," Mom yells out, "answer the phone."

I pick up the receiver. It's him. Didn't he tell Mom he needed a few days? I guess he's changed his mind.

"Abby?" he asks.

"Yes?"

Silence. Filled with awkward agony.

"This is Naveen." Pause. "Your..." Pause. "...dad."

This is so *wrong* in infinite ways imaginable.

Nobody should have to have this conversation. Your first hello to your father comes the minute he cuts the umbilical cord and cries tears of joy. And you're covered with bloody goop and your mom is passed out from exhaustion. You don't say hi to your dad for the first time ten minutes before you get on the bus when you're in eighth grade.

My dad wants to Skype. He thinks it might be easier if we can see each other. He apologizes that he couldn't get on the next plane. His mother—my grandmother—is sick.

I tell him we can Skype that evening.

We set up a time and I hang up. It's probably the strangest conversation I've ever had.

Introduction to Dad via Skype: 8:00 p.m.

Dad, could you make sure you wear a shirt? I want to say. Ha! Of course I don't.

I had a board book titled *We Are All Different* when I was little, with bright colorful drawings. Our stories are different too. Are there as many stories as storytellers? Is there a book in the library about first meetings with dads? The how-tos?

The Skype connection that evening is grainy and echoey.

Mom tries to act nonchalant and fails. "So should I call you Kabir or Naveen?" she says, followed by strangled laughter.

"Naveen's fine," my dad replies. "The whole world calls me that, even my mother."

He wears a shirt. He looks different from Internet Dad—a bit tired, and he has stubble. His eyes still wrinkle when he smiles. And he touches his ear when he searches for words like I do.

He looks—well—normal.

"Abby, Meredith," he says, "I am so sorry. I don't know how this would have worked out if I'd known. But I know it would have not been like this. I know that for sure."

A smile of relief lights up Mom's face. I struggle to keep it together.

Who am I? he wants to know.

A normal teenager who loves the violin and was raised

by a single mother? A girl who tried soccer but hated it? A girl who occasionally thinks in rhyme and has an imaginary string quartet?

Who is he?

A man who wants to make up for the lost years and get to know his daughter.

"Abby, I want to meet you. This Skype thing is so fake. I wish I could hop on a plane. But I can't right now with your grandmother in the hospital and my shooting schedule and a big movie premiere coming up."

All these words are so strange. *Grandmother. Shooting schedule.* I've heard of shooting ranges but not of shooting schedules. Movie premieres happen in Hollywood, and I guess Bollywood. Abby Spencer doesn't hear about them. Nobody I know mentions them. Instead, we talk about upcoming birthdays and plans for long weekends.

And then, as if the whole thing isn't weird enough, he sheepishly asks, "Meredith, Abby, does anyone else know about this?"

"You mean about your mother?" Mom is usually smart. I guess we all have our duh moments.

"You mean about you being my father?" I jump in.

"Yes," my dad says. "I told my publicist and he wants to think about the best way to release this information to the media."

Publicist, media, press release! Whoa!

"Oh! Oh!" says Mom. "My parents and Susan, my business partner, know. I realize that our lives will change once the world knows. Abby, you haven't told any of your friends, have you?"

"Priya and Zoey know. But I told them to keep it a secret because I need time to figure things out. They would never tell anyone unless I said they could."

"Abby, Meredith, could we keep this quiet a bit longer? Please?"

After we sign off, I can't help thinking that having a daughter is a skeleton in my dad's closet. Except I'm not a pile of dead bones. I'm living and confused by it all. The string quartet wails.

❧ CHAPTER 9 ❧
BACON IN YOUR CUPCAKE?

Zoey decides we have to meet at the Yogurt Cup the next day since my allergic reaction started it all. They want to hear more, hear all.

This time I choose mango with white chocolate chips as the topping. As I approach the coconut, I dance away in mock fright. Zoey steps in as a human shield between the coconut and me. Priya provides the sound effects of the ambulance siren blaring and the da-da-da of a horror movie. Priya covers her yogurt with coconut in honor of its major role.

Counter Guy laughs. "Hey, glad you girls came back. Thought you might boycott us forever. You," he says, pointing at me, "scared us that day."

Zoey grins wide enough to show her molars. I drag her away, afraid she'll scare him.

"So, your mom wrote him a letter and he didn't get it," says Zoey when we sit in a deserted corner.

"That is so tragic," says Priya. "Like a movie or a book."

"Yup, my life would make the best book," I reply.

"So you think the letter got lost or do you think someone hid it from him?" Priya's eyes are the size of bottle caps, her voice all dramatic.

"I don't know. My grandfather died the next year, so I guess we'll never know." All this is so strange, it belongs in a Ripley's Believe It or Not.

Priya bursts in, "OMG, Abby, does this mean that you are rich and famous? Naveen Kumar is like a big deal in India."

"No!" I say. "No! Don't be ridiculous. Nobody knows him here."

But I wonder, would I be rich or famous because my father is Naveen Kumar?

Priya breaks the silence. "My mom suggested I have a Bollywood-themed birthday party this year."

I almost choke. *Get outta here!* A week ago, Bollywood didn't figure into my world and now it's splashed all over. Figure that!

"It was so weird after what you'd told us earlier. I said it was the lamest idea I'd heard," Priya says.

If my father had turned out to be a plumber instead of a Bollywood star, I'd think it's a brilliant idea.

"You don't think your mom knows, does she?" I ask, scared. "I have to keep it a secret. My mom and my father are worried that the media will hound us."

"I thought that too. But no, she doesn't. There's no way she could."

"I trust you both *completely*. It can't be leaked," I say.

"It's a pact. We swear to not say a word," Zoey says as we hold hands and giggle.

"A pact needs blood," I say.

"No blood," says squeamish Priya. "I'll faint."

"Okay, how about we smear yogurt on our fingers and swear secrecy?" I suggest.

Zoey is the first to follow through. She dips all five fingers in her yogurt cup and we form a circle with our hands and touch the tips of our fingers. I have too much yogurt and it ends up trailing down my arms. Oh what a sticky mess of secrets we are. After we rush to the bathroom and wash up, we look at pictures of Priya's newly born niece and walk home. I'm more relaxed than I have been for days, and for once don't have a headache.

The minute I enter the house, Mom looks up from her computer, frazzled. "Abby, your father called. He wants to Skype again in an hour. I don't know what's going on. He said he had been up all night at the hospital with his mother."

"I have to shower," I say.

"Abby, we have to respect his request. Give him some time. He's just found out he's a father. That is huge. I had months to prepare after I found out. And he's a celebrity—we don't understand the complications of his life and work—and he's trying to protect us too. Or maybe it has to do with your grandmother."

The possibility of the Skype call being related to a sick grandmother I've never met makes me feel guilty.

Why can't my father be an engineer or an accountant or a janitor? Why does he have to worry about media and red carpets?

Mom and I watch an episode of *Cupcake Wars* while we wait for my dad's Skype call. We wail at the ingredients (zucchini, salted peanuts, bacon, rice) the poor contestants are asked to put into their cupcakes. In their place, I'd say, "No can do."

An hour later my dad calls. Funny how fast I've started calling him my dad. Maybe it's because he's always been Dad in my daydreams. I try referring to him as Father at times and Dad at other times depending on my mood. Mom says something about it. Calling him Father seems weird, like I belong to the British aristocracy. Father, the palace is a bit drafty today, eh?

Even though I call him Dad, he doesn't feel like he's my dad yet.

I ask him the question that's been on my mind. "So why did you change your name?"

"I changed my name to Naveen because there was another actor named Kabir at the time," he explains. "Naveen is my middle name. Your grandmother was the last one to switch to my new name."

Then my bleary-eyed father makes a request as unexpected as adding bacon to cupcake batter. "Meredith, I know I'm asking a lot, but could Abby come to India? To Mumbai?"

Excuse me? Wailing violins! What did he say? Did I hear that right? I look over at Mom.

Mom and I stare at each other and then at the monitor. Mom keeps gulping.

Before either of us can say anything coherent he says, "Hear me out. My mother is doing better. Last night she was so sick, I thought I might lose her. I was overwhelmed and emotional and told her about Abby. She was shocked at first, but then she perked up." My father shakes his head, looking stunned.

Mom says, "But…"

"God help us all," he laughs with a tinge of panic, "she wants to meet Abby. She seems to have summoned the strength to live to meet her." He continues, "We haven't talked about what my dad might have known yet. But she was genuinely surprised when I told her. Her big regret has always been that she didn't have any grandchildren, which is why I believe she had no idea about the letter you wrote."

I say, "But…"

"What do you think, Mere? A short visit? I'll send her a ticket, of course," he hastens to add. "I would invite you too, but I'm sure you are busy with your café."

"Oh, absolutely," my mom agrees. "And I could not impose on your mother right now."

And it would be majorly awkward.

Then it gets even weirder than adding bacon to cupcake batter.

"Well…" says Mom, tugging at the hem of her sweatshirt and tapping her foot rhythmically. She has a sheepish look on her face. Would she agree?

"Thanksgiving is coming up, and Abby has a week off from school. She does have a passport." Last year, we applied for a passport for me, thinking we might go to Mexico.

Mom looks at me begging for help!

"I don't know, Naveen. She's so young and the journey to India is so long and…" Mom's voice trails off.

"I'm thirteen, but I don't even know you," I interrupt.

My father takes a deep breath. "I agree, Abby, but that's not my fault. It's no one's fault," he adds. His voice is hypnotic and comforting but with an edge. "But I've missed out on much of Abby's childhood—isn't it time we get to know each other? Skype is a poor substitute, don't you think?"

How could anyone disagree with that?

"And if your grandmother wasn't so frail, I wouldn't ask," he adds.

That is the clincher. I can see Mom's expression soften. Her own parents mean so much to her, and she knows my dad's mom means as much to him.

"Meredith, don't worry about the travel. Abby will go first class, and I will arrange for the airline to escort her. One of my friend's kids traveled to the U.S. from Mumbai and it all worked out," he cajoles.

Mom and my father talk for a while. Mom raises all her doubts and he appeases her. I exhale and start to breathe again.

They decide. I, Abby, will go to India next week.

Should I scream with excitement or be terrified? The string quartet is confused too.

My father is jubilant. Mom and I don't know what to do after we hang up.

"I'm going to India to finally meet my father and my grandmother, Mom," I say uncertainly.

"I know, honey, and I'm happy for you," she says, smiling.

"But I've never gone to a foreign country and I'll be alone," I say, nervous.

Mom raises her chin. "And you're a smart girl and you'll be fine." Her tone is determined, as if she's off to wage a war.

Is Mom trying to convince herself?

Mom tells Grandma and Grandpa Spencer and they react with all the questions Mom had asked my dad. This time she uses all the answers that he gave her to calm their fears. I tell my friends and again swear them to secrecy and promise to tell them everything and email and text. They are super duper jealous.

Two days later, I stand in line clutching my paperwork at the Indian Visa office with Mom. It's a sparse room, the posters on the wall providing the only color. *Incredible India!* they read. Some are a bit faded and curled at the corners. The Taj Mahal blinks at me, as does a mysterious woman in a red sari.

I wonder if my father was acting or was it real when he said he felt bad about not having been part of my childhood. He sounded so sincere. Does he really want to get to know me? He must love his mother to go to all this trouble.

I was angry before, but now I can't be angry with him. He isn't a deadbeat dad. He just didn't know.

He is an actor though; it's what he does for a living. Is it all an act?

This is going to be such an adventure. I ride the roller coaster between thrill and terror.

The woman at the window stamps my passport. Bang! "Have a great trip!"

It's too late to question the ball rolling down the hill.

My father's "people" have already talked to Mom and gotten dates. The ticket is booked.

My people—Mom, Grandma, and Grandpa—are scrambling. There is so much to do!

Father and his people say, "Don't worry about anything. We'll take care of it!"

But Mom worries.

She frets about packing clothes and taking medicines and being in a foreign culture and traveling for more than twenty-four hours on my own and the shots I need and my cell phone working in India and granola bars and pudding cups in case I don't like the food.

"Abby, I've packed two pairs of jeans, do you think that's enough? Do you think it's okay to wear sleeveless shirts in India? I wonder if it's hot in November. Maybe I need to call Naveen and clarify the clothing dos and don'ts."

We go back and forth about my violin and in the end, I decide I have to take it. I can't go without practice for ten days.

I worry about everything my mom is worrying about too. But mostly I worry that my father and I won't like each other. It could be a huge problem when father and daughter meet so late instead of at birth. Babies are all so cute and adorable that all dads love their babies.

At thirteen, I have a zit on my nose. I don't have headgear or anything tragic like that, but I'm a metal mouth. My knees are dry and gray. I have opinions about people and canned versus frozen peas, music and T-shirts. If I don't wash my hair every day it looks stringy and ugly.

What if he thinks, "*She* is my daughter? Nah! Not feeling the love"?

⊱ CHAPTER 10 ⊰
HICBUCROAK!

I belong in first class like a bull belongs in a china shop. To make matters worse, I catch a bout of incurable hiccups as soon as I find my seat. The flight attendant fusses over me, bringing me water, orange juice, and Sprite. I sip each one.

No. Effect. On. Hiccups.

They sound like a cross between a hiccup, a burp, and a mating bullfrog. *Hicbucroak!* So elegant! I want to hide under the seat with the flotation thingy.

The flight attendant says taking off my sweatshirt might make me feel cooler and possibly get rid of my hiccups. I take off my sweatshirt. And freeze.

The flight attendant gives up and walks away. I swaddle my blanket around me and press the satin-edged corner over my mouth to muffle the sound. My string quartet plays a lurching song and keeps in beat.

Hicbucroak!

I try to sleep.

Hicbucroak!

To take my mind off my hiccups I look around my rather posh surroundings. I'm in first class because my dad is rich. Does that make me wealthy by association?

Apparently, my dad has a big film coming out soon. His career hinges on it. His people don't want controversy or any focus on his personal life to affect the opening weekend. He is a single star in his mid-thirties, and no one expects him to have a teenage daughter. Doesn't exactly go with his image. Who'd have known the existence of Abby Spencer could derail a big budget Bollywood blockbuster? I should feel powerful, but I don't. Hicbucroak!

The premiere is at the end of my stay, the day before I return. I'm missing three days of school before Thanksgiving break. We keep the official story for the world simple. I was invited to India by one of Mom's college friends—half-truth. My dad is Mom's friend *from* college. Mom isn't going with me because Thanksgiving is the busiest time of the year for Slice of Muse—truth.

To distract myself, I do some makeup homework. In language arts, we have to write our life story.

My life story is not what I thought it was. It's a construction zone roped off so no one falls in and gets hurt. Does that make my life story prior to the big reveal a lie? Possibly.

Hicbucroak! That one had the volume turned up. I give up and put away my assignment.

The flight map on my monitor is hypnotic. The plane is a little ant flying through the skies leaving behind a path of dotted lines. Kind of like Hansel and Gretel leaving bread crumbs. The plane is circling around Boston and almost out of the States. I will it to move faster.

The longest flight I've been on was from Houston to San Francisco—in coach. No one offered me hot mushroom soup with homemade croutons on that flight. All I got was a bag of pretzels and a soda!

Maybe it's the rich mushroom soup or the refined air in first class or me thinking about my revised life story. Maybe it's the first flight on my own or saying good-bye to Mom and Grandma and Grandpa at the airport. Or maybe it's the thought of meeting a stranger called Dad, but I feel queasy.

Maybe suffocating my face with the blanket to muffle the hicbucroaks was not such a good idea. The air pressure in the plane pounds against my head.

At the airport before I left, Mom handed me a pill for motion sickness. "Abby, it's a long flight and Priya's mom thought you might need this. So take it." I slipped the pill into my pocket and I thought I'd take it if I needed it.

I should've taken it. I needed the medicine thirty minutes ago. I need to rest my spinning head. One minute the soup sloshed in my stomach and then the next it was in my throat.

Frantic, I search for the barf bag. There isn't a bag, only an in-flight magazine selling fake rocks to hide your speakers in the garden.

Jeez, do passengers not get sick in first class?

The soup sloshes its way up my digestive track. I reach for the blanket and the rest is history. The woman sitting next to me shrieks and sits on the flight attendant buzzer. She didn't pay upward of five thousand dollars to sit beside a girl who makes hicbucroak sounds and throws up into a blanket. The flight attendant calms her and moves her to another seat. She finds an unsuspecting glamorous Indian woman to occupy the seat beside me.

I've never been so embarrassed. Physically I feel better after chucking up. The barfing realigned by body's internal organs and magically cured my hiccups. Yippee!

After a quick wash in the miniscule capsule pretending to be a bathroom, I change into pj's.

Yes, the nice flight attendant gave me pj's!

Airline's huge hint to Abby Tara Spencer, *Shut up and fall asleep!*

The plane now inches toward Europe. I didn't want to be sick again. I take the tablet Mom gave me and conk out.

Hours later, I wake up over the edge of Africa. The cabin is dark. The woman beside me looks less glamorous with her head lolling to the left and emitting a barely audible snore.

My stomach growls in protest.

The flight attendant with the smiley freckled face sees me and comes over. "You missed dinner. We'll serve breakfast in a few hours. Would you like a snack?"

I nod. She comes back with peach yogurt and granola, which have never tasted so good. After being asleep for so long, I'm wide awake. Everyone on the dimly lit plane is asleep while I read my travel guide to Mumbai. It's a present from my grandparents. The cover is a photo of the Gateway of India. Soon my brain is buzzing with facts—like how Mumbai was originally a group of islands and that the city is India's economic and commercial center. It's India's most diverse, cosmopolitan, and westernized city.

The flight map on my TV console says we're over Afghanistan. It feels weird to be flying 30,000 feet above a war zone. Same space, different altitudes, and different stories I think as I page through my book.

Finally the captain announces that we're about to begin our descent into Mumbai International Airport. I gather my belongings, tighten my seat belt, and pray through the bumpy landing. The plane shudders, sighs, and touches its wheels to the earth in exhaustion.

"Good luck," The flight attendant squeezes my hand as I get off the plane, my backpack over my shoulders and clutching my violin case. Because I'm an unaccompanied minor, an airline employee with immaculately creased pants meets me at the gate.

For the first time in my life, I'm in a foreign country. My string quartet is quiet as if it too wants to hear all the foreign languages spoken around us. The sounds are gibberish to me interspersed with familiar nuggets of English. Huge rusty fans swing on pedestals, valiantly fighting the heat. Surrounded by newness, I struggle to take it all in. Women in saris walk all around me—some are travelers like me while others are airport staff. There are other people dressed like me in jeans and shirts.

At the immigration desk, I say I'm visiting friends. What if I tell them the truth? Would the earth stop revolving? Would it be like a scene in a comedy when chaos rules? I grin, imagining an elephant running through the busy airport, clearing desks with his tusks and crapping in the gift shop.

I look at my watch as the immigration officer checks whatever it is immigration officers check. It's eleven a.m. in Houston. What is Mom doing?

He stamps my passport with the seal for entry. Thunk! He slides it through the window.

My airline chaperone hustles me through customs and out of the airport terminal. The sliding doors open, and hot, humid, pungent, dark night air sneaks into the airport to cool down.

I scan the faces behind the rusted metal barricade. It seems like hundreds of men are holding up signs for the passengers they're meeting. I disregard the signs and focus on trying to locate my father's face.

Right to Left. Left to Right. I've never seen so many people milling around at this hour at an airport. Mumbai, I read, was the most populous city in India—with a population around fifteen million. It's the fourth most populated city in the world, and I'm sure a good chunk of those people are at the airport!

My eyes scan the crowd. A crumb of panic rises. I look at the signs. None of them reads *beloved long-lost daughter.*

A car honks and startles me. My backpack slides off my shoulder. The heat swirls around me. The smells of sweat, heat, soil, and people overpower my brain.

My chaperone tugs my sleeve and points to a sign. "There."

A man holding a sign with my name sees us point and steps forward, "Abby?" he yells.

Who is this man? Why isn't my father here?

The airline employee and the man discuss. The man signs some papers and then my chaperone says good-bye and leaves.

"Wait! He's not my father." Sheer panic invades my body, down to my smallest pore.

The man hands me a cell phone.

I hold the phone to my ear. "Abby! Welcome to Mumbai," my father's voice booms.

"Dad?" I ask. "Why aren't you here?"

"I didn't think you'd want the hoopla after a long journey. Thomas is my publicist. He'll drive you home. I'll see you in thirty minutes."

I hand the phone back to Thomas, give him a weak smile, and trip over a mangy dog sleeping on the street.

"Sorry, guy," I whisper to the dog, whose bones stand out against his skin, and follow Thomas to the waiting car.

✤ CHAPTER 11 ✤
MY DAD IS BIGGER THAN YOUR DAD

A white-haired Indian man opens the car door for me.

"Abby, this is Shiva," Thomas says.

I hold out my hand, but Shiva joins his hands and does a slight bow. "Namaste."

I feel stupid. Next time I'll do a namaste too.

We get into the car—me in back, Shiva in the driver's seat on the right, and Thomas in the passenger seat on the left. Thomas turns on the air-conditioning and then chuckles. "You thought Naveenji would come to the airport? Do you know what *hangama*—chaos—that would cause? There would be photographers going mad and fans fighting for autographs."

His tone is condescending.

I have to focus to understand his accent. "Oh, I didn't know," I say.

"You didn't know?" His laugh is disbelieving as if I'm an idiot. I already know I don't like this man much.

"You didn't know," Thomas repeats, unbelieving. "Naveen Kumar," he says with pride, "is the king of Bollywood! He has acted in thirty-five movies. Each one has been a hit. They have each grossed over a hundred crore rupees. He has millions of fans. Women love him and want to marry him. Men? Men are jealous of his body. They wish they had his charm. Kids mimic his dance moves." Thomas's voice rises in ownership and I cringe.

This guy thinks I'm an ignorant idiot who lives under a rock. Shiva pulls the car into traffic, and we drive on the "wrong" side of the road, which I guess is the right side here.

"In India, Naveen Kumar is a phenomenon. He is big. Bigger than the prime minister!" Thomas voices his declaration of love.

Finally he looks at me. "You must be tired."

My watch says it's noon in Houston, and the clock on the dashboard of the car says it's 11:30 p.m. in India. I've been traveling for more than a day. Mom, Grandma, Grandpa and I left home for the airport almost thirty hours ago. No wonder I feel like a plant that hasn't been watered for days. I slept, but not enough. I rest my head against the tinted window of the air-conditioned car.

Keep your eyes open, Abby!

I struggle to take in my surroundings through the haze of fatigue. It's dark outside. The streets feel smaller and dustier than at home and there seems to be a lot of construction near the airport. Then we're on a highway. I look out at the buildings on the side of the road and force myself to stay awake. I see an exit sign that reads *South Mumbai* and under it is a script in an Indian language.

In spite of my efforts, my eyes close.

"Naveen Kumar is big in India, big, big, big…" Thomas's voice echoes in my sleep.

My head whacks against the window and my eyes fly open. The car lurches with a thud. At first, I think I'm still on the plane and we've hit a turbulent patch. But then I realize we've just propelled over a pothole.

"Shiva, drive carefully!" Thomas chides.

I look out the window. We're not on a highway anymore. We're on a smaller, crowded street and I can see groups of people gathered around. There seems to be some kind of celebration on the sidewalk. Music blares and people dance.

A giant billboard of a man looms over us, like Gulliver over a Lilliputian city. I look at his face. It's my father's!

I gasp. "Is that—?"

"Of course.," Thomas replies. "It is his big movie. The premiere is in eight days. Very soon. This movie is the best,"

Embarrassed, I turn back to look again. I can see the back of the billboard, a twin image of the front. My dad, at least fifty feet tall, striding with a menacing look like Arnold Schwarzenegger in the *Terminator* movies. He wears a ripped sleeveless T-shirt, so ripped down the front that he might as well not be wearing a shirt. His muscles bulge, his face is streaked with dirt, and he appears to have survived some grueling escapade to hell and back.

I want to shut my eyes. No, better yet, maybe I could paint a shirt on every poster of my father in this city.

"*Jhoom*—that's his latest movie. It's the first one that we have produced under our production company. By God's grace, it will be a huge hit," he says, crossing himself. "Bollywood will be at his feet."

Thomas's belief in my father is touching even if the publicist is crazy. When he's excited, he talks even faster.

Focusing on Thomas's accent and trying to stay awake is making my head hurt.

We turn onto a road with the ocean on one side—the Arabian Sea to be exact. Mumbai is a peninsula surrounded by the ocean. I crack the window just a bit and I can hear the waves pounding the rocks.

All along the drive I'm surprised to see what looks like large, brown sandbags on the sidewalks and under bridges. What are they for? When one of the sandbags gets up and starts walking, I'm shocked. My heart constricts. It's not a sandbag—it's a person.

I see now that people sleep on the streets, under the shadows of skyscrapers, with threadbare sheets pulled over them, their knees in the fetal position. Cocooned in their homelessness. I read that Mumbai is both a city of dreams and of extreme poverty. Some sources in my book claim that one in five people in Mumbai lived below the poverty line.

"We are almost home." Thomas shakes me out of my wandering thoughts.

I've anticipated this moment all my life. Meeting my father, the person who made me. My hands are clammy and my mouth feels dry. This is, of course, nothing like I thought because my imagination hadn't flown me halfway around the world.

The car slows in front of a fifteen-foot wall that hides most of the house behind it from street view. All I can see a small curved balcony on the second floor. On the other side of the road, the pitch black Arabian Sea roars. I have goose bumps on every inch of me. Even at this late hour, a group of people is gathered outside the gate. I wonder who they are. Tall, ornate gates swing open without a creak and the group rushes to get a glimpse inside.

Our car glides in. My heart beats faster than the speed of light. The gates close behind us.

The car stops in the driveway, and I step out of the car, clutching my backpack.

The front yard is paved with slate tiles, and a fountain stands quietly in the center. Red bougainvilleas pour from huge lush pots that line the wall. An ivory house with modern-looking stucco sits in front of me. It has an enormous, ornately carved front door with brass knockers. The outer walls are like a fortress keeping out the rest of the city. It feels like a completely different world.

The night air is humid and I'm dizzy with excitement. I'm barely aware of the flurry of activity behind me. Thomas runs to get my luggage, a man in uniform emerges and nods at me, and yet another man opens the front door.

He steps out—my father, in flesh and blood. Real, in this unreal moment.

The father whose absence has defined my life, whether I like it or not.

The string quartet soars.

I remember all the moments when I yearned to know him. At Doughnuts with Dad, at father-daughter dances, in family pictures, and across the kitchen table each evening for dinner. The wait is over. This moment will always divide my life into before I met my father and after I met him.

He stands with arms outstretched. He's wearing jeans with a white T-shirt. "Abby!" he says.

For a moment I'm paralyzed.

Dad? Could this be happening? Or is he a hologram?

He comes toward me and I step into his arms. Maybe there should be awkwardness but there isn't. Strangely I feel safe.

In that moment he becomes real. He becomes my dad.

"Dad!"

Then he holds me at arm's length and looks at me. His eyes mist. He blinks and brushes his eyes.

"Wow! You look like a clone of Meredith with dark hair. You take me back years!" he shakes his head in disbelief.

Thomas and Shiva hover around. Dad thanks Thomas for meeting me at the airport, and he leaves. Shiva, I learn, lives with Dad.

We walk into the house. It's unreal. The floors are lined with silk carpets, huge windows and cathedral ceilings make the space light and airy, and the sound of sea waves provide a natural sound track. Tall bamboo plants with their waxy leaves sit in gleaming bronze pots. Museum quality bronze sculptures of Ganesha and the Buddha adorn various corners. The beautifully blended décor is at once ancient Indian and modern. I'm no art dealer, but the stuff on the walls scream real!

I've never been to a movie star's house before, and now the one I'm in belongs to my dad. Crazy! I'm certainly not in my middle class, homey house in Houston anymore. I read that Mumbai is the wealthiest city in India and therefore a magnet for people seeking a better life. People from rural India come to Mumbai every day to try to find job. I've seen both the poor and the rich within minutes.

Before I can absorb anymore of the house, Dad says, "Abby! I know it's late and you're exhausted, but you have to meet your grandmother. She refused to sleep. She had to meet you."

I'm surprised. It's past midnight. I expected to see her the next day. I know she lives with Dad. Mom explained that in India elderly parents often live with their children.

Dad leads me through the foyer into the living room. An elderly woman sits in a cozy-looking armchair, watching TV. She's dressed in a loose-fitting blue tunic that grazes her knees over matching loose pants.

As soon as she sees us, she rises to her feet. She holds a cane for support in one hand and the other hand reaches out to welcome me. Dad rushes to steady her weak, shuffling gait.

"Abby, I had to get better. I had to meet you." Her English is deliberate and accented.

I've been worried that she might speak only Hindi. She lets go of her cane, holds my face in both her hands, and kisses my forehead. Happiness lights up her eyes.

"Grandma Tara, it's nice to meet you," I say.

"I like that name. Grandma Tara," she repeats and smiles at Dad and me. "You say it differently than we do, but I like that, you know."

"How do you say it?" I ask. When I say Tara, it rhymes with Sarah.

"Ta-ra." She says it with a soft *T* and it rhymes with Lara. I say it her way.

Grandma Tara laughs. "No. Say it the Abby way."

Shiva steps forward. "You have to rest," he says.

Grandmother waves him away. "Seeing my grand-daughter doesn't tire me," she says in a regal voice. The she turns to Dad and they speak in Hindi.

"She says you are beautiful, and she's glad she didn't die," Dad translates for me. He shakes his head and bursts into a huge guffaw of laughter. He raises his hands and claps. Genuine happiness pours out of his smile.

I shrug away fatigue. Oh, I am glad too!

☙ CHAPTER 12 ☙
NAMASTE

Weird trivia learned in Science: experts who know stuff say that human babies learn more in their first year than ever again in their life. I can argue with that. Like a baby who has entered a new world, I've learned new stuff every minute since I left home on my own. The sights, sounds, smells, tastes, Dad's presence, and Grandma Tara's hugs are all brand new.

"Abby, wake up," I hear Dad's muffled voice as he knocks on the closed bedroom door. "Your mom called to check on you twice already." After all my traveling and family introductions, I crashed and slept forever like Sleeping Beauty.

I struggle to open my eyes and emerge from my sleep marathon. I'm in India—in Mumbai! And I wasted my first morning sleeping! I jump out of bed and smooth my bedhead. I open the door, and Dad steps in. It feels a bit weird. He's my dad, but he's also a stranger.

"Abby, I hope you slept well," he says.

I assure him that I did.

"I want you to be careful to not drink any unbottled water," Dad reminds me. "It's not safe, and you can't fall sick on my watch. Use bottled water to brush your teeth and don't drink the water when you shower." Then he smiles. "It's good to have you here. I'll see you when you are ready."

"Give me five minutes," I say to his retreating back.

Last night I was too exhausted to take in my surroundings, now I soak them in. Sunny, almost sheer cotton curtains hang from the windows, which have wrought iron grills on them. A window unit air conditioner hums. Everything is different. My bed is a twin and has a futon-like mattress covered with a pink and green paisley cotton sheet. Instead of a comforter, there's a softer sheet more suitable to the weather. It's not Houston hot, but the temperatures are in the low eighties and it's still humid. Dad says I'm lucky; the temperature is cooler than usual.

There's a wardrobe across from my bed, like the one in the Narnia books. The tiled floor feels cool under my feet. A patterned cotton area rug sits between my bed and dresser. The cream walls are concrete. There is a picture on the dresser of Grandma Tara, a young boy, and an older man.

I walk into the slate-tiled bathroom. I need more light. I can't find the switch then remember seeing a panel with several unmarked switches on the bedroom wall just outside the bathroom. I'm not sure which one turns on the bathroom light and I end up turning on the two lights and the fan in the bedroom before I find the bathroom switch. The toothpaste—neem flavor, which tastes woody—and the sandalwood-scented soap have a tropical feel. The water doesn't gush out like at home but is more of a medium-speed stream.

As I step out of my air-conditioned room onto the landing, the temperature changes. The windows are open and the sheer curtains flutter in the breeze. The house doesn't have central air.

A crow outside screeches, "Caw!" I can hear the gurgling of pigeons on the windowsills and the hum of traffic. The house sits on Carter Road, which faces the ocean. Across the street, no more than five hundred feet away, I can see craggy, coal-black rocks, which merge with the loud ocean. I step to the window and soak in the sight of the ocean hurling itself at the rocks.

"I love the waves. It's why I bought this house." Dad steps out of his room down the hall and joins me.

"I would rather hear the waves than the hum of my air-conditioning unit," I say.

"In November, that may be true. I turned the unit on in your room so it felt more like your home." He turns from the window to look at me. "My team is waiting for me. They come over quite often, especially when I am reading scripts or doing interviews or photo shoots. I want you to meet them."

We walk down a spiral staircase with a polished wood banister that opens onto the impeccably decorated first floor. A group of people waits in the living room.

"This is Abby," Dad says. "Her mom, Meredith, was my best friend when I studied in America. This is her first time in India."

Smooth introduction, Dad. Back then Mom was your best friend? I guess you could say that! I feel a little twinge of annoyance but brush it away. I wonder who knows I'm Naveen Kumar's daughter and who doesn't. Obviously, not everyone does. I want my parents to hurry up already and tell the world, but the saner part of me knows it's easier for me to not be the focus of media attention as I get to know Dad and Mumbai.

Remembering last night, I join my hands and say namaste. They all say hi.

Jeez, I'm going to get this right before I leave!

But Dad beams at my namaste. "Abby, you know Thomas," he says, indicating his publicist.

I nod.

"And this is the rest of my team—Shankar, my hair and makeup whiz, Asin, my manager, and Salima, my gatekeeper."

I remember Salima. She is a worthy buffer—it took Mom weeks and multiple calls to get through her. Even the way she drapes her long scarf around her middle says efficient.

I'm meeting my father's peeps. I'm familiar with a few Indian names thanks to Priya; otherwise, I'd be totally lost. I still struggle to remember all the introductions.

Dad turns and talks to the gang. He switches from Hindi to English and back to Hindi. Now I get it, now I don't, now I get it, now I'm lost!

It's like *Hinglish*, a curious combination of Hindi and English like Spanglish is a combination of Spanish and English.

"*Hanji*," I hear them say a lot between head nods. "*Hanji*."

They continue to do whatever they were doing before Dad and I arrived, and Dad takes me into the family room through a corridor lined with pictures of his career.

"What does *hanji* mean?" I asked him.

"Oh! They mean yes, sir. *Ji* is a respectful suffix."

"They said that a lot."

"Did they? Sometimes I feel like all I hear is no or *nahi*!"

Grandma Tara sits in a rocker next to a couch and a love seat, watching TV. Across the seating arrangement are windows that look onto the backyard. Shiva sits with her. They both turn toward me with huge smiles.

"I go to see you room," Shiva says slowly and then turns toward Dad and speaks fast in Hindi. The way Shiva says my name it sounds like he's saying A-B. I'm probably saying some of their names all funny too.

Dad laughs. "Shiva says your grandmother sent him to your room a dozen times to check on you to see if you were awake. He also apologizes for his English."

"Oh, I'm sorry for sleeping forever! Please tell Shiva that his English is miles better than my Hindi so he doesn't need to apologize."

"Abby, we'll eat in an hour. I'm listening to a pitch for a new movie script today in my home office. I'll leave you with Grandma Tara and Shiva. They've been waiting to take care of you. While you're here, you can teach Shiva English, and he'll teach you Hindi." He reminds me to call my mom before it's too late at night in Houston. Then he's gone.

Mom answers on the first ring. "Abby, how are you? Did you sleep in? How was your flight? How is Naveen? How is his mother? Oh, Abby, it's so good to hear your voice."

"I'm fine, Mom, really I am. It's so new and different though," I whisper.

Mom's questions soon become less frantic. Before we

hang up, we decide that she'll call again in a couple days. She seems so far away. I miss her already.

"You hungry?" Shiva asks when I re-enter the living room.

Grandma Tara worries that I haven't eaten in too long. "Airplane food!" she says with disdain. "It's not fresh."

Shiva and Grandma confer.

Shiva is a small man, maybe an inch shorter than my five-foot-four. His wizened face has pockmarks I hadn't noticed last night, and his white hair is thinning. He reminds me of a taller, thinner Yoda.

"I like paneer," I say when he asks whether I've eaten Indian food.

Shiva almost dances with joy. "You know paneer? Shiva makes best paneer for Abby." He skips back to the kitchen. I can make Shiva happy by asking him to cook for me? That's easy!

I sit with Grandma Tara. She strokes my hand as she watches her Hindi soap opera. I have no clue what the actors are saying. But the soap operas have the same melodramatic sound track in India as back home. How many violinists do they employ?

Seeing Grandma Tara's wrinkled hand with its thin skin holding mine, I realize that now I have two grandmothers. She looks so frail. I'm glad I'm meeting her.

I look around at the room, which is so different from

the living room in my house. Speckled tile covers the floor. The decorator didn't make this room a showcase like the living room. It feels homier. The sofas are squarer and not as padded or as big as the ones at home. There's a dresser against the far wall covered with a crocheted runner. A set of little elephants stands on it. A garlanded picture of an older man, the same man from the picture in my room, hangs on the wall. Is he Dad's father and my grandfather? Did he hide the letter Mom wrote to Dad?

When I tell Grandma Tara that Mom and I made an album for her and Dad, she wants to see it immediately. She summons Shiva. He in turn calls two giggling women, Mina and Bina. More help? Priya's mother explained that middle class families in India have help and it provides employment. Mina and Bina are Shiva's sous chefs and general go-to girls.

They appear to be twins. Priya and I dressed as Thing One and Thing Two from *The Cat in the Hat* one Halloween years ago. Mina and Bina with their rhyming names and shy smiles remind me of Priya and me.

I have quite the audience. Grandma Tara and I sit on the couch and Mina, Bina, and Shiva stand behind us.

"Mina and Bina think you're very pretty," Grandma Tara says, searching for the right words and gesturing at me. They ooh and aah over my baby pictures and I blush.

At lunch, the house feels like a party. Dad and his

team emerge from his office and join us. Between Dad's people, Grandma Tara, Shiva, and the two women, we are a lot of people. I look around the table and beam. I realize I don't have to wonder about my dad and his life anymore. Here it is, sitting around the table in his swank dining room.

I'm an American with my accent. In a room full of people who speak Hinglish, I feel like an outsider, even though I know half of me is Indian.

Mom would say, give yourself time to adjust to your new reality, Abby.

I run to my room to get my camera. I ask Dad to take a picture of me with Shiva, who stands ramrod straight and is totally embarrassed. I post the picture of me flanked by Mina and Bina in their saris. Then I post another close up of their earlobes. They wear little earrings all the way up the cartilage.

Shiva insists that he take the group picture of me with Dad, Grandma, and all Dad's peeps.

I take pictures of everything, even the matar paneer.

I post the photo and add a caption: *The best in the world. It melts in your mouth.*

I'm having a ball and accidentally say Dad when I'm talking to him. Dad catches it and gives me a look, reminding me that my parents still have to figure out how to break this news. I shake off stressful images of my very private mom's world being invaded.

After lunch, Dad takes me for a drive. It's the first time I'm stepping out in broad daylight in India. Again, the crowd is outside the walls.

"Naveen Kumar," they shout as we drive out. Dad stops and signs a few autographs.

The ocean waves seem calmer in the afternoon. People are walking along the seawall, some in traditional clothes, others in running shorts.

We leave the sea and drive along a winding uphill road to what appears to be a market area. Vendors sell fruits and vegetables along the streets. Part of the street is blocked for construction. An array of shops sits alongside one another. A doctor's office is next to a shop selling snacks. Next door is a shop with a man frying something in a huge wok. My senses take over. I've never seen so many people within inches of cars and rickshaws. I'm terrified that Dad will hit human, animal, or thing.

I see children with bare feet and tattered clothes playing tag by makeshift homes. They approach our car at the stoplight, begging for money. I've seen the occasional adult ask for money at home, but I've never seen children who seem to have so little. Dad can see I'm upset. He rolls down the window to awed shrieks of "Naveen Kumar!" and hands out little bags of biscuits. "Your grandma makes these and always has them in the car." The expression on his face says he wishes he could do more.

I don't know how to react and the stoplight turns green.

The stray, mangy dogs rummaging through garbage is a sight that will be seared in my memory.

Across the street, a tall apartment complex gleams, polished and new.

"Abby, Mumbai's contrasts, the poverty and the wealth, can be difficult. You have probably never seen hardship like this at home. Do you want to talk about it?"

"Dad, I don't know where to start. The kids…" I say and stop. I can't find the words. Dad understands. "Know that you can come to me."

My eyes pop at the next intersection when I see a cow coolly sitting and swishing her tail in the middle of the chaotic street.

She's slimmer than any cow I've seen at home, but there she sits in the middle of the road, the undisputed queen of her kingdom. Traffic weaves around her. Google already told me cows are sacred in India.

"Welcome to India," Dad says.

In that instant I open the window, throw my fears out, and click a picture.

We drive past an open-air bazaar. Fresh vegetables and fruit are piled on handcarts. The greens, reds, and yellows of the saris flapping in the wind are irresistible. "Dad," I yell, "slow down, I need to take another picture."

I realize that Dad's house and style of living is not typical of the rest of India. It's as if I'm living in the Trump Tower in New York. I haven't seen this kind of poverty and neither have I experienced the wealth of my dad's lifestyle.

೩CHAPTER 13೩
FRIENDS OLD
AND NEW

The next morning, rested and energized, I go downstairs to a quiet house. Dad is away, shooting a new film, and his entourage is with him. I thought we were supposed to spend time together. I've waited thirteen years and traveled halfway across the world—8,000 miles in a yucky airplane—to Mumbai, and he can't take some time off to spend time with his only daughter?

Grandma Tara rests. She's tired after yesterday's excitement. I can hear Shiva, Bina, and Mina's voices from the kitchen and go looking for them.

"Namaste," I say as I walk in.

Mina looks at Bina for approval then says, "Good morning," in her accented English. Then she bursts into giggles of embarrassment.

I giggle back, partly embarrassed by the way they all jump to attention whenever I walk into a room.

The bougainvillea vine outside the kitchen window is a riot of pink. The roar of ocean waves and the sound of occasional car horns waft through the open window. People here, I realized yesterday, honk whenever they want with little guilt. The open windows also bring in the humidity. The temperature is in the low eighties. While this street is not as busy as the market we drove through yesterday, it's way busier than the streets I'm used to in my neighborhood.

The kitchen counter has almost fifty gleaming stainless steel cups arranged on trays. The morning sun glints off the cups, almost blinding us.

"What are these for?" I ask, pointing to the cups.

Mina and Bina giggle again. Shiva gives them "the look." It's funny how "the look" is the same across cultures! My mom has given me that same look many times.

"I tell after breakfast," Shiva says.

"Indian breakfast?" I ask, my stomach growling.

I realize that Shiva has as much difficulty with my accent as I have with his, and we communicate best when I keep my sentences short and speak slower.

Serving me elaborate meals makes Shiva feel like he's doing a great job. Who am I to rob him of the satisfaction? Shiva, Mina, and Bina wait on me like I'm in a full-service restaurant.

"*Upma* for A-bby," says Shiva, setting a plate before me.

"U-p-ma?" I repeat. I take a small bite.

Hmm. I take another bite. It reminds me of a cross between grits and polenta but with an Indian flavor. It has peas, onions, and cashews in it. I'm an adventurous eater so I dig in.

"So what's with the cups?" I ask again, pointing.

Shiva says the fans stand outside the gates of Dad's house 24/7 for a glimpse of him regardless of the weather. Most days Dad steps out, signs autograph books, and obliges fan requests for pictures. Shiva tells me many are tourists; some are people from India's rural areas. In their eyes, Naveen Kumar is God.

I like the way Shiva talks about Dad's status better than the way Thomas tells it. Somehow, it doesn't sound all braggy.

"Fans like guests. Sometimes, God comes knocking at your door like a guest," says Shiva.

"I take them water at noon," he says.

I'm intrigued by Shiva's status in the house. I figured out that he's the driver, head chef, and general housekeeper. He didn't drive Dad to the studio today because he stayed home to take care of Grandma Tara and me. Dad is obviously okay with giving him that responsibility.

"I remember my days," Shiva mumbles to himself.

"What days?" I ask Shiva, curious.

"Nah!" he says. Not one to sit idle, Shiva picks up a basket of snow peas and sits down on the stoop outside the kitchen door. It opens onto the lushly landscaped backyard. Tall coconut trees, blooming rosebushes, and potted plants surround an impeccably manicured lawn. A covered swing seat sits on the slate patio. It all looks like it belongs in a magazine spread. I can imagine Shiva serving Dad and Grandma Tara tea out there.

Shiva scoots to make room as I sit by him. One by one, he squeezes and pops the shells and pulls the peas out. I shell too. Peas for me have always come in a bag from the freezer. After much coaxing and insistence (Please! Please! Please!), Shiva reluctantly tells me that almost forty-five years ago he came to Mumbai from his village in northern India as a teenage runaway.

"Shiva, you were about my age," I say. I can't imagine being alone in a gigantic city like Mumbai.

Somehow, in spite of our language barriers, Shiva and I communicate. He tells me how he escaped drought and poverty in his village. When he came to the city, he eked out a living as a shoeshine boy. Shiva has a faraway and pained look in his eyes as he talks.

Then he waves away his memories and smiles at me. "No sad talk," he says.

I want to know more. "How did you meet my grandparents?" I ask. "That's not sad, is it?"

The word *grandparents* feels new when I use it to refer to my father's family. Grandparents have always been Grandpa and Grandma Spencer.

Grandma Tara's husband, my grandfather, used to come to him for shoeshines and took a liking to him. "What do you want to do?" he asked the young Shiva.

"Abby, my dream to drive car," Shiva says.

My middle-class grandparents paid for Shiva's driving school and then gave him a job. He's been with them ever since. He's like family.

I squeeze his hand. I want Mom, Grandma, and Grandpa to meet my new friend. "Will you come to America, Shiva?" I ask him.

He laughs. "No, no! I no English!"

Even Mina and Bina, who hover in the kitchen, eavesdropping, understand. They tease Shiva in Hindi. I understand the word *America*, even though they pronounce it Ahm-ri-ka, with an emphasis on the *Ahm*.

"You come to give water?" he asks me.

"I'd love to." I grin.

I lifted one of the trays and follow Shiva. The wiry security guard at the gate grins and asks Shiva in Hinglish if I'm his assistant.

"*Hanji!*" I reply before Shiva gets a chance.

They all smile at my effort to speak and understand Hindi. I love the way they root for me.

There are around thirty people from different walks of society gathered outside. They are united by their fandom. I'm offering water to a fan, admiring a canvas portrait of Dad that she painted, when I spot a seriously legit cute boy.

Darn. I'm wearing a sloppy ponytail—not my best look. And I wish I'd worn something cuter. I'd thrown on some baggy Bermuda shorts and a T-shirt. My forehead shines from the humidity.

"Mom, how long have you known Naveen Kumar?" I hear him ask his kurta-and-jeans-clad mother in a totally American accent. I stare.

"Before he was Naveen," she laughs.

"So from the dinosaur days?" he jokes.

I think the boy is around my age. He wears shorts and a T-shirt with the words *I breathe cricket*. Even cuter at second look.

His hair flops on his forehead, almost covering his huge brown eyes. Eyes that crinkle with wicked laughter. His smile is an eleven on a scale of ten. He's gangly tall, like he'd grown last night.

I smooth my T-shirt. As if that would transform it.

This could be an Abby-meets-cute-boy moment. My string

quartet plays a hyper jig. But I can't meet a cute boy wearing a scrunchie. I pull it out and fan my hair. I have standards.

Shiva greets Cute Boy's mom and they chatter in Hindi. From the way he greets her, she's obviously an expected guest. I bet they're saying, "Sorry, I'm late. The traffic was a mess."

They laugh and yada-yada some more in Hindi.

I stand there, not sure what to do. Should I talk to him?

Before I can decide what to say, he turns to me, "Hey, I'm Shaan," he says. "They're catching up. Mom used to live next door to Naveen Kumar when they were kids. She always visits Tara Aunty when we're in town."

"I'm Abby. You understand Hindi?" I ask.

Duh, of course he understands Hindi. Didn't he just translate?

"Yes. Yes, I do. And English." He's laughing at me. "And you?"

"Oh, I speak English. But I don't speak Hindi." Genius, Abby.

Shaan's cell phone buzzes and he reaches into his pocket. He grins as he reads a text. He sweeps his hair off his forehead and types an answer.

Shiva and his mom are still talking animatedly. I look down at the tray in my hand and decide to continue passing out the water. I peek at Shaan as discreetly as possible. Cute. Definitely cute. He continues to smile as he types. I stare, knowing he's texting and not looking at me. Then he looks up and catches me. Oh Schmit!

I turn away red-faced but then can't resist a peek back.

He bows. Oh Schmidt again.

I smile. He'd been looking too. My stomach somersaults. I struggle to focus on my task. For the first time I truly understood Zoey and her crushes.

"A-bby," Shiva calls, and I hastily finish handing out the rest of the water. "We go inside."

"Holy crap!" Shaan blurts out when he steps into the house and earns a look from his mother.

"I know, right?" I say.

Grandma Tara is thrilled to see Shaan's mother. "You have met our special guest, Abby. Her mother and Naveen went to university together in America."

"Is this your first trip?" Shaan's mom wants to know.

"Yes," I reply. "And what about you?"

"We visit every other year," Shaan says. "We live in Dallas, but my grandparents live in Mumbai."

He lives in Texas? My stomach somersaults again.

Shiva rushes off to make chai and Shaan and I wander toward the wall of Dad's pictures.

"So have you met Rani yet?" Shaan whispers in a conspiratorial tone and points to a picture of Dad with this completely dazzling woman.

"Who's she?" I ask.

"Get outta here!" Shaan exclaims loud enough to grab Grandma Tara's and his mom's attention.

"Rani was Naveen Kumar's heroine in *Kismet.*"

Seeing the blank look on my face he elaborates, "*Kismet* was only his biggest hit ever. They are the hottest couple of Bollywood."

Grandma Tara purses her lips at the mention of Rani.

I struggle to control my conflicting emotions. Shock, disappointment, interest. What did I expect? Of course Dad had a hot girlfriend! Do the tabloids combine celebrity couples' names in India too? Are they the Raveen of Bollywood?

Shaan's mom tactfully changes the topic, "If you haven't seen *Kismet*, you really should. Shaan's cousins are taking him tomorrow. It's been running at the Mandir Cinema for five years, hasn't it?" she asks Grandma Tara.

Even Grandma Tara agrees that I should go.

"You have to come with us. We'll have a great time. We'll educate you," says Shaan with the goofiest grin. The grin makes me want to smile all the way to my toes. I wonder if my hair is a mess. Why couldn't I have known I was going to meet him when I threw on my clothes this morning? I'd been thinking of the temperature and humidity—so unimportant when the cutest boy ever enters the scene.

Shaan and his mom leave after she takes some pictures

with Grandma Tara and Shiva for old times' sake. I take some too. I want a picture of Shaan to show Priya and Zoey.

☙ CHAPTER 14 ☙
LOST IN TRANSLATION

Dad calls Shaan's mom that evening and they catch up. Yackety-yak. He thanks her for including me in their movie plans. "Abby will love the movie on the big screen. Thanks for inviting her. Maybe you and Shaan would like to join Abby when she comes to my movie set the day after," he suggests before hanging up.

My eyes bug out of my head. I'm visiting the set of his movie? Squee! Why didn't he tell me? With Shaan? That might be more excitement than I could handle. I might spontaneously combust.

Over dinner, Dad tells me the story of the movie I'm seeing the next day so I'll understand. It's in Hindi, of course, and there are no subtitles. "It is a typical Bollywood boy-meet-girl story with action, and song

and dance thrown in for flavor like bay leaves in curry,"
says Dad.

"Or like blueberries in muffins," I add and he laughs.
"BTW, where did you meet Rani?" I ask.

He looks at me intently. "On a movie set many years ago.
We've acted in seven movies together."

I hope for more. Are they in love? Does he plan to marry
her as the old magazine I found in the bedroom claims?

All he says is, "You'll meet her when you come to the set
tomorrow. I hope you're not bored—"

"Bored? You're joking, right?"

So I would meet Rani too. This is getting interesting.
A movie set, a day with Shaan and Dad, and a surprise
ingredient—Rani! Wow!

Dad laughs with his eyes. "We're shooting a song. I
thought it might be more interesting for you than a dramatic
scene. So much of filmmaking is sitting around waiting for
the shot to be ready."

I called Mom immediately to tell her about the movie
plans and the set visit. "Honey, what a glamorous life you're
living. Have a good time."

"Mom, it's so cool. A week ago I'd never met him, and
now I'm going to his movie set."

Then I tell Mom about the not so cool—the children
begging at traffic lights, the homeless sleeping on the streets,

and the stray dogs and how Shiva and I fed them rotis. "From the number of rotis we have, they're not all leftovers. Shiva makes a few extra to feed them. We are pals, Shiva and I. Oh, and, Mom, I've been playing my violin for everyone. They call it Concert Time and they think I'm the best ever!"

Mom laughs and says, "Abby, how exciting this trip is for you!" Then we say our good-byes and hang up.

It is exciting. A small voice whispers, *exhausting too!* Everything is so different. The feel of the mattress, the kids playing cricket on the streets, the coolness of the floor, the sound of the ocean, the temperature, the sea breeze, the different rupee bills and coins, the sounds of Hinglish, the taste of Thums Up—Indian Coke—the game of carom that Grandma taught me, and the awful fishy smell the wind sometimes brought in from the fishing village a few miles from Dad's house. It's all so new, there's always something to learn and something else to photograph. Then the little voice says, *Abby, you wouldn't want to change a thing. You're having a blast.*

The next morning, Shiva walks me over to the apartment building where Shaan's cousin lives. It's about a block away from Dad's house. Shaan's cousin, Jay, greets Shiva and me with an angelic namaste when we enter the sixth floor apartment. He's in his twenties and his hair is all wild. He's our chaperone/

driver to the movie and will drive us for pizza afterward. He jokes that he'll tuck us in bed and read us a story too!

He messes Shaan's hair and then he reaches over and pinches my cheek as if I'm five! Really? I'm lobster red.

Shaan's mom and Shiva both wave good-bye to us with huge grins as we step into the elevator. I guess that this is how non-movie star, middle-class people lived.

We ride down to the first-floor garage.

Jay walks over to an awaiting motorcycle and says, "Abby, you ride with me."

I look at the motorbike and think, *Seriously? You told Shaan's mother you were driving us—like in a car. This has to be a joke. Mom will kill me if she ever finds out.*

The string quartet plays a da-da-da tune, warning me of danger. "And what about Shaan?" I ask.

Seemingly out of nowhere another bike thunders.

"This is my friend, Ravi. You ride with him," Jay says to Shaan.

"Really? Cool!" says Shaan, jumping onto the bike and putting on his helmet.

Jay hands me a helmet and guns the bike. Its loud, animal echo in the garage makes me jump. "Get on."

What is going on? I swear only minutes ago Jay was a candidate for parents' pet of the year with all his hand-folded namastes.

The whole scene reminds me of a thriller in which a gun-toting international spy lurks out from behind a concrete pillar and start chasing us at any minute. I peek over my shoulder. Before I can censor the words, they spill out of my mouth. "Is it safe?"

Jay puts on his helmet. "Mwah! Ha! Ha! C'mon, kiddo, of course it's safe." He guns the bike's throttle again and bends over the chrome handlebars, "Get on, or we'll be late."

I stand there.

"C'mon, Abby," Jay yells over the roar of the bike. "Trust your elders. Get on," he thrusts the helmet at me.

Elders? Jay is twenty-something and acts like an immature twelve-year-old.

"I've ridden with him before," says Shaan. "He's okay." He doesn't seem to have my reservations.

Against my better judgment, I put on the helmet and get on the bike. I don't want to be the dork.

We shoot onto the streets of Mumbai like a cannonball.

Would Dad approve of me going to the movie on a bike with crazy Jay?

"Hang on!" Jay yells.

Do I have a choice? Not if I want to live.

The bike roars on the street alongside the ocean. The wind flaps my scarf across my face. As the wind picks up, Jay's laugh sounds more maniacal and makes me dig my fingernails into his shoulders. Finally I clutch his middle with my arms and hold my breath. The string quartet is so frightened it fumbles notes.

We weave through the streets of Mumbai. This time I feel exposed on a motorbike rather than safely inside Dad's car. We snake through rows of cars strangled in traffic. I gape at scooters with entire families on them. I've never seen so many people—except maybe after a football game. It seems like the streets of Mumbai are always busy. Cows, dogs, the occasional goat, and humans all share the road with trucks, bikes, motorcycles, rickshaws, and cars. Makeshift shanty shops coexist with bars and restaurants that would fit in New York. Old, derelict buildings stand alongside shiny chrome and steel skyscrapers that house corporate offices and ritzy malls.

The slums of Mumbai sprawl from its sparkling ocean. The muddy color of poverty is interspersed by the bright blue color of the tarpaulin people use to keep the rain out of their homes.

We're always within less than an inch of something. Jay's driving paralyzes me with fear—even my gasps are silent. We screech to a halt at a traffic light and I hesitantly look up to see that Shaan is next to me. He grins and I begin to melt inside. But then I catch a glimpse of something behind Shaan. There it is again, the poster of shirtless Dad—his abs displayed for the world to admire and for his daughter to die of embarrassment.

I suggested to Dad that he should always have his shirt on since it embarrasses the heck out of me, his thirteen-year-old daughter. He threw his head back and laughed, but Grandma Tara was my ally. She smiled. "Naveen, I agree with Abby."

To make matters worse, Jay points at the display of abs and laughs. Shaan mimics tearing his shirt off. My face is so red it could explode.

The light turns green and we rocket off again. Ready, set, vroom-vroom. Are we competing with someone? Now the road is uphill. Skyscrapers loom around us. The sea sparkles to our right again, the sun's rays reflecting diamonds on the water. The ocean is never far, always around the corner.

In spite of myself, I relax a bit. This motorbike tour of Mumbai will be a secret, always. If I tell Mom about it, she would be on the next flight over. And I do not want that.

Since I've been here, Dad has forbidden raw fruits and vegetables. I drink nothing but bottled water. Shiva lights mosquito coils in the house after sunset. As Dad said, I would not fall sick under his watch. No Delhi belly for me! But here I am motorbike thrill riding with a maniac.

Jay slows down to point to the dome of the Haji Ali mosque in the ocean. "We're almost there!" he shouts.

The motorbike purrs like a cat when we slow down and park. I get off on shaking knees and pull off my helmet with trembling hands. Shaan gets off Ravi's bike, comes over to me, and whispers, "Abby, let's keep this a secret. If my mom knew, she would kill Jay and me." He grins. "But let's take a picture to show our friends."

Shaan and I exchange a pinky swear. "Our parents will never know," I promise.

Ravi takes a picture of Jay, Shaan, and me with the bikes in the background. Priya and Zoey would never believe *this* story without evidence.

"I have seen this movie three times already," Jay says as we cross the parking lot. "But for you guys, I'll watch it again."

I can't even answer because there is shirtless Dad *again*. Larger than life cutouts of Dad stand in front of the theater. Fans clamor to take pictures with the cutouts.

Jay leans in. "You guys want a picture?"

"No!" Shaan and I say together.

I whisper to Shaan, "I'm going to paint a shirt on him."

He gives me a funny look. "Why? You against fab abs?"

Oops. Not sure how to respond to that without an explanation. I give a weak fake smile.

People stand in a line that crisscrosses the theater for tickets. Jay preordered the tickets and we buy something called masala popcorn and walk in. Shaan explains that the popcorn is flavored with an Indian spice mix. I pop one in my mouth and taste the newness. Hmm! Nice spicy smell.

The lights dim and ads came on. I have an aisle seat, and Shaan sits next to me. Neither of us uses the armrest between us. I'm scared to invade his territory. Is he? We're so close, one move, and I'd brush his arm.

The credits roll. *Starring Naveen Kumar* flashes across the screen and the audience claps enthusiastically. I can feel obvious excitement. I've never seen someone I know— let alone my dad—projected larger than life on a gigantic screen. Just the size makes him seem somehow unreal. Yes, I saw the billboards, but this is different. He's moving, talking, dancing, and I can see every pore on his skin. Weirdville. He's speaking in Hindi, which I don't understand, but I can tell from his expressions and the reactions of the audience around me that he's a good actor.

Fifteen minutes into the movie, Shaan relaxes, leans over, and claims the armrest. He leans toward me, his face close to mine. I almost jump and spill my popcorn. What is he doing?

"He's coming on to her in this scene," he whispers, his lips less than an inch from my ear.

Seriously? Why is he explaining this? It's so obvious even without knowing what they're saying that a newborn could figure that out.

But instead of saying anything like that, I whisper, "Do they get together?"

I shiver and feel goose bumps on the arm that leans against Shaan's.

Shaan continues to translate and whisper into my ear while I blush in the dark.

He explains each nuance in the plot and I play along like I have no idea, even though Dad already told me the story. But Shaan doesn't need to know that.

Shaan's breath is warm against my ear, and he smells of pinewoods and breath mints. The warmth of his breath tickles my stomach. My skin burns where our jeans touch.

On the screen, Dad woos Rani. In the theater, my translator teaches me the language of flirting. At one point Dad looks straight into the camera and directly at me. I almost say, "Shaan, my dad's watching!" But I catch myself.

Nothing—nothing—could've prepared me for the first song-and-dance sequence. It's like the one we watched on International Day. Except it's not. That was on a computer monitor and this is on a big screen. Every shake of Dad's hip and every flicker of his eye are magnified. It's an MTV video but bigger than all of us, and the rhythmic music wants to own our souls. The audience sings along, taps their feet, and roars their approval. Even Jay, who was asleep beside Shaan, wakes up.

I get into the spirit, clap, and hum along. Shaan's eyes connect with mine in the dark. Embarrassed, I look away. Shaan gives a Coke burp. We giggle as if it's the funniest thing ever.

The string quartet celebrates by joining in and playing the song from the movie.

Please don't let the movie end ever, I pray.

৬ CHAPTER 15 ৯
HOLY COW!

The movie does end. Harsh lights replace the magical, whispering dark. Abruptly Shaan and I move apart. Shaan sticks his hands into his pockets and I tie my purse string into an unnecessary knot. Jay asks us all, "Who's hungry for pizza?"

We walk over to a pizza place across the street. I didn't expect to see Pizza Hut or McDonalds or KFC in India, but here they are.

Jay orders chicken tikka pizzas and we settle into a booth and dig in. Yup, the pizza has chicken tikka as a topping instead of pepperoni. And it is yummy!

Shaan says, "Hey, Jay, doesn't *mandir* mean temple in Hindi?"

"Yes, it does. I'd never thought about the theater being called Mandir Cinema."

"Well, in that temple, Naveen Kumar is god!" Shaan declares with his mouth full.

"And Rani is the goddess, isn't she?" Jay and his friend drool over Rani.

My thoughts drift away.

Before I went to middle school and decided I didn't need a father, I often wished that my dad would come and whisk my mom and me away. Not on a horse or anything, but drive up in a car. I know it was a silly crazy *Parent Trap* notion. Happy neat endings only happen in Disney movies. I scold myself, *Grow up, Abby.*

But it was such a perfect daydream that I couldn't help myself. Dad would come over and meet Mom, and they would fall for each other all over again. Maybe they would whisper in the dark like Shaan and I did at the movies. Mom isn't dating anyone so that isn't a problem. Why did Dad have to be dating this horrible, beautiful Rani creature? Bollywood's Brangelina! Hrumph!

I bite into my yummalicious piece of pizza.

What would Dad think of today's Mom? He told me he was impressed that she ran her own business.

Yesterday after Concert Time Dad became a bit mushy. "Your mom did an amazing job raising you on her own. I'll always owe her."

Grandma kissed me on my forehead, said something in

Hindi, and then went to bed.

"What did Grandma say?" I asked Dad.

"She wants the evil eye to never fall on you."

Dad and I continued to sit on the antique wood swing outside. Its broad wooden seat was polished smooth with use and the carved brass ropes on which it was suspended told stories.

"Hey, Abby, why the smile?" Jay asks, bringing me back to the present.

"Oh! I'm thinking of dessert," I lie.

"Have you tried *kulfi*?" Shaan asks. "It's an Indian ice cream."

An hour and a pistachio *kulfi* later, Jay jumps to his feet. "Do you guys realize the time? I promised my girlfriend I would meet her at six! She hates it when I am late and I was late twice last week. Three strikes and I may be toast. So we better hurry back. Ravi, follow me."

I think he just wanted an excuse to drive crazy. He jumps on the bike and I hurry after him. Here we go again! I clutch his shoulders and he guns the bike. It's a busy intersection and hordes of pedestrians cross the street when the traffic light turns red. Even crazy Jay has to stop.

Jay swears at the traffic. "We'll never make it at this rate. I'm going to take a shortcut," he says and swerves off the road into a smaller back alley, and I feel like I'm stepping through a portal into the belly of Mumbai. Shaan and Ravi follow. This lane is so different from the main road we've left.

Nothing I've seen at home could have prepared me for how little some people have in this world. Shops in large raised corrugated tin boxes line one side of the road. On the other side stand makeshift structures built of tin, mud, and plywood. They are people's homes. This is not the street where Naveen Kumar lives. I cling on for dear life, bug-eyed. Children with bare feet and bare torsos run around, chickens peck at garbage heaps, and a goat bleats. Naked yellow light bulbs light the street, and exposed electric lines hang overhead. It strikes me that my mom didn't count on me seeing this India. It wasn't featured in any of the tourism brochures.

Shaan and Ravi catch up to us. Even Shaan has lost his grin. Then their bike lurches over a gigantic pothole and swerves to avoid colliding with Bessie the cow. Or maybe in India she's called Latika.

My hand flies to my mouth to muffle a scream. The bike slams onto the road. Startled Bessie-Latika says, "Mooooooooooo!"

The string quartet amazingly moos in harmony with Bessie-Latika.

Pedestrians scream.

The kids stop playing and gawk.

Even the chickens freeze for a second before they scurry away.

I hear Shaan's uncensored version of oh Schmit!

Jay slams on his brakes and turns around.

The other motorbike has spilled, and Shaan is sprawled on the street.

My heart pumps as fast as a Vivaldi concerto. A million thoughts compete in my mind. Is Shaan okay? Please, God, let him be okay. Almost instantaneously, as if they sprung out of the earth, hundreds of people gather, speaking in a foreign language, yelling.

Shaan leaps up, shaken but with only a skinned elbow.

In the dwindling light, the fallen bike, Shaan's elbow, the throng of people, and the shadows paralyze me. My heart is beating so loudly that it seems to dwarf the rest of me. I've never felt more homesick or alone. I want my mom. I want to be home.

"You guys okay?" Jay asks Shaan and me.

We nod.

"Let's get out of here," Shaan says, nervously scanning the growing crowd.

Ravi punches Jay on the arm. "You idiot! What's wrong with you?"

"I thought we would get home faster if we avoided the main road," he answers.

Jay says to Shaan and me, "Some of the people who work in our homes live in these neighborhoods."

I think of Mina and Bina and wonder if they live in similar neighborhoods.

I can feel hundreds of huge eyes staring at us with unmasked curiosity. Among a sea of Indian people, my paler American skin stands out like a white shell on a brown sand beach.

Luckily, nobody is hurt, not even Bessie-Latika. The police arrive in a jeep. Jay apologizes and explains. Shaan and I stand and shiver. I try to hold back my tears. I can imagine myself in an Indian police station.

Luckily, no harm was done and the police ask Jay to leave. We hastily get back on our bikes and find our way back to the main road and to sanity.

Jay rides as sedately as possible the rest of the way home and I can't have been more grateful. He apologizes a million times when we reach home.

Shaan apologizes too. "I usually like Jay's crazy stuff, but today he scared me. I'm so sorry."

I walked into the house, shaken, with my hair disheveled from the wind. Grandma Tara and Shiva look at me with puzzled expressions. "Did you leave the window open in the car?"

Oh! They'll never know, will they?

"Yes, is it a mess?" I say, acting innocent.

"Abby!" Dad calls from his room. "Can you come upstairs? I have news. I need to talk to you."

"Give me a minute, okay? I want to wash up," I yell back.

I race up to my room, close the door behind me, and stand against it, taking long breaths. I want to pick up the phone and spill the beans. Tell someone about the movie, Shaan, the shortcut, the fall, and crazy Jay. I can call Mom, but I can't really tell her much besides the movie part. She'd have a complete meltdown. My stomach flips, thinking about my afternoon.

I call Priya. She's been to Mumbai so she'll get the picture. I need to unload or I'll explode into bits like a melon crashing to the floor.

It's six o'clock in India. It's 6:30 a.m. in Houston. Time to wake up, Priya!

Groggily Priya gasps. "No! You're making this up. OMG, Abby, glad you're safe. You cannot tell your mom."

"Abby!" I hear Dad yell.

"Uh-oh, Priya, I really need to go."

"I can't believe all this stuff is happening to you." I can almost see Priya shaking her head.

"I know. I'll tell you more later. Bye!" I get off the phone, rush to the bathroom, washed up, and pull a brush through my hair. I have to look normal. Dad can't know about the ride. He'd be livid.

Can a just-discovered dad ground you?

❧ CHAPTER 16 ❧
GATEWAY TO DAD

Dad sits in the living room with his feet on the coffee table, his fingers knitted together behind his head. His entourage hovers around him, competing for his attention. Someone wants him to approve an outfit for a photo shoot. Someone else wants him to look at a shooting schedule. The third person wants to know if he can attend the opening of an exhibition. And the fourth one begs him to attend the wedding reception for the daughter of the minister of broadcasting.

I want to spend alone time with him. I can't say that though. It would sound so lame.

Dad sees me slink into the room and sit on the rocking chair in the corner. I could be a fly on the wall. I catch my breath after my literally hair-raising ride. Dad fends off the demands, saying yes, no, and maybe without faltering.

Maybe it's years of practice. I take longer to decide which top to wear with my jeans. "No to the wedding. It will take me two hours to get there in Mumbai traffic," he says. Then he calls, "Abby!" and draws attention to the fly.

"Everyone," he looks at Thomas, Salima, and the rest of the gang and says, "I'm taking the evening off. Yes," he cuts off the groans and protests with a slicing wave. "I'm taking my"—he stumbles—"Abby out to dinner. Work will have to wait."

I think he almost said "my daughter." I swear. My heart skips a beat.

He walks over to me, puts his arms on my shoulders, and looks into my eyes. "Abby, give me ten minutes to freshen up. We're going to the Taj for dinner. Thomas, tell Shiva I plan to drive myself."

Dad's dejected entourage files out of the room.

I grin as if I've won the first prize in a talent show. "I'll go change too."

My book told me that the Taj is a famous, grand old hotel, and I want to look appropriate. I also know by now that wherever Dad goes, paparazzi follow. I want to look nice.

Grandma Tara looks as pleased as a mama bird that caught a worm when Dad and I say bye to her. "Naveen," she says, "show her the Gateway of India and maybe take her for a boat ride on the harbor. Abby, I want you to have a good time, *beta.*"

I know *beta* is a term of endearment and that it literally means son, but it's used for both sons and daughters. Grandma Tara has been using it to refer to me for the last two days. Shiva smiled when Grandma first said it to me. Once I knew its meaning, I smiled too when she said it.

Having said our good-byes, we get into Dad's Mercedes. What a day it's been. First the movie with Shaan, then the ride with crazy Jay, and now this dinner with Dad. If the rest of the days are this eventful, I could pack a lifetime of excitement into this trip.

As we drive, I realize this is the first time that Dad and I are completely alone since the short drive the first day I spent in Mumbai. Strangely, I'm tongue-tied. While I miss home and Mom, I feel like a dry sponge absorbing everything I can. Making up for lost years.

My mind whirls like one of those diagrams of brain synapses in my biology book. Zing, zing, zing! Thoughts, words, feelings all clash and collide and I'm mute and a bit choked up. I can't cry! No way.

Dad puts in a CD and startles me with the sounds of Beethoven's *Concerto no. 5.*

I stare at him in surprise. I didn't know Dad likes Western classical music.

"I know how much the violin means to you, so I bought some CDs," he says.

He's taking an interest in *my* music—for me.

"Thanks, Dad," I say.

Our eyes meet. "You're welcome, *beta*," he says. I get goose bumps. "Abby, I wanted to talk to you about this secrecy."

"It's okay. It's fine," I interrupt, not wanting to spoil the moment.

"No, no it's not," he says, his hands clenched on the steering wheel.

Silence. The violin swells in the car. In spite of myself, I smile. No one could have planned a better sound track if they tried. Seeing me smile, my dad smiles too. He exhales as if he's been holding his breath. The car is at a traffic stop and he mimics playing an intense piece of music on an invisible violin. I pick up my imaginary violin and join him in the crescendo. Is there a term for air violin like there is for air guitar? Well, we're doing a heck of a job air violining to Beethoven!

What seemed like a million people cross the street. The traffic light turns green. Dad puts down his imaginary violin and so do I. We grin at each other as if we're the only two people on this planet that matter. I'll never forget this moment for as long as I live.

We drive on the Worli Sea Link, picking up speed. The Sea Link is a brand-new twenty-first century toll road suspended over the ocean. We stop at the tollbooth. The man almost falls off his perch when Dad rolls down the window to pay.

"Naveen Kumar!" he says in a choked voice and elbows his partner. Without looking, the partner says, "Naveen Kumar? In your dreams!" but then sees that it is indeed Dad. He leaps to attention and salutes Dad as if he were a general. Dad chuckles as we drive off.

"Abby." He takes a deep breath. "Your mom and I have been discussing how best to reveal that you're my daughter. I have to be the one who makes the statement. I've scheduled an interview and photo session with *Film World* on Friday. The editor is a friend of mine and has been supportive from the beginning of my career. I told her you are my daughter but not that we just met. That is too personal and nobody's business."

I'm not sure how to react.

Dad continues. "The editor promised that she would handle the story as respectfully as she can without distorting it. The issue will hit the stands a week after that."

"I'll be home by then. Will you mail me a copy?"

"You know I will," he replies. "My film premieres this weekend. Abby, for the first time I'm responsible for the entire film. It's a subject close to my heart. The hero is a TV reporter who investigates and uncovers corruption. I want the attention to be on my work, not my personal life."

"And I don't want the attention and neither does Mom."

"I understand, but it can't be a secret forever. And I don't want someone else to discover and distort the truth."

We're both silent as we realize this has to be done.

"Your mother and I will figure out the details in case anyone tries to contact her. I'm sure she needs to tell some of her friends and family too."

I still hate the idea of the press trying to contact Mom. It didn't strike me that someone could twist our story, my story. I've watched my share of *TMZ* and *E! News* at home. The hosts of the show are always wondering about the personal lives of stars.

Will Brad and Angelina marry this summer?

Which Kardashian is having a baby this year?

I guess there's an equivalent of *TMZ* in India and I might be the subject of its speculation. Why did I never think of that? The hosts could announce:

Why did Naveen Kumar hide his teenage daughter?

I shudder.

Dad looks over at me. "Abby, you understand, right? I don't want this to be made ugly and sordid."

I nod.

Why did Naveen's girlfriend hide his child from him?

Is she really even his child?

More disgusting headlines creep into my mind like roaches crawling out of the sink. Dad sees me wince and says, "Abby, don't worry about it. I'll take care of it. It's why I was hesitant to tell people. I want to be in control of how it's spun."

Now I feel like an ignorant brat for ever doubting the reason Dad wanted to hide my identity from the press. He's trying to protect me.

We're driving through a part of Mumbai with old Victorian buildings from the British era. Some are lit up and the coconut trees around them wish they're as tall.

"The old Churchgate Station, Flora fountain," Dad points out. They are magnificent and centuries old, which I'm not used to. America is such a young country in comparison.

Dad swings the car into the foyer of the Taj Mahal Palace Hotel across from the Gateway of India and hands the keys to a valet who gapes in surprise and recognition. The last speck of sun lazily lowers into the ocean. The Gateway stands tall and majestic, with its turrets and latticework, its stone lit by the sinking sun.

Impulsively Dad grabs my hand, "Let's go see the Gateway. I haven't gone up close in years." He slides on his sunglasses as if to hide his face.

We cross the street, leaving behind stunned onlookers in our path. I can hear the whispers of "Naveen Kumar" echo around us. We run through the pigeons and tourist photographers. The Gateway official recognizes Dad and waves us through. We read the plaque: *The Gateway was built to commemorate the visit of King George V and Queen Mary in 1911.*

"And when the British left India, the last ships to leave for England also left from the Gateway," Dad adds. "I'll have to tell you about India's history and colonial rule sometime, Abby."

The words are a promise that we'll know each other for a long time, and I almost skip along. I haven't been sure how my relationship with Dad would be. There are kids who don't see their fathers in years. I've been living in the moment, afraid to imagine a future with Dad, but now, who knows? He's said other stuff, how he'd like to come and be at my orchestra concert sometime. Maybe we'll visit each other.

Maybe he'll come to Houston. I can just imagine introducing Dad to my friends and to Grandma and Grandpa Spencer. I pinch myself. How crazy and fantastic would that be?

A small crowd has gathered. Dad whispers, "I think we better head back inside before the crowd grows too big."

Dad poses for a few photographers and asks one of them to take a picture of us against the backdrop of the Gateway. Then, Dad and I manage to weave out of the gathered fans and run across the street. I can't help waving at a few of the fans who are waving at us.

The Taj Mahal Palace Hotel with its stone façade looks over at the sea. We walk in and enter a palace from another time. Soft sitar music pipes through the hotel. My string quartet joins in. A fusion concerto.

The air is hushed and air-conditioned. Marble floors and exquisite murals make me glad I changed my clothes from what I'd been wearing on the back of the motorbike. This is as different from the back alleys as McDonald's is to a five-star meal. I remind myself that my book said that Mumbai is India's wealthiest city and that it's ranked higher than Shanghai, Paris, and Los Angeles on the number of billionaires who live here. In a matter of hours, I'm seeing both sides of the city and I feel like Alice in Wonderland when she goes from being miniscule after drinking potion to huge after eating cake.

We stand at the host stand and a manager walks over, beaming. Her sari rustles and she greets us with a dazzling smile.

"I hope I can get a table at the Shamiana," Dad says,. "I don't have a reservation."

"You are always welcome, sir," she says and whisks us away to a table. Dad and I feast on kebabs and naan and every other delicacy possible. The chef comes out to suggest items on the menu. We're treated like royalty. Dad orders dishes he thinks I'll like. He makes a point to tell the chef that he and I are allergic to coconut and asks him to make sure that none of the curries have coconut milk and that coconut is not used as a garnish.

A shared dinner. A shared allergy! Shared interests? A shared life?

When we're alone, Dad says, "Abby, would you like to go shopping to prepare for the photo shoot? Or you can wear your jeans and I could match you?"

"I want to buy an Indian outfit for Priya's birthday party. Maybe I could wear it for the photo shoot too?"

Dad laughs. "As many as you want, *beta*. I'll have Salima take you. Or maybe Rani, if she has the time."

My stomach flip-flops. Shopping with Rani? Seriously?

"Grandma Tara would love to take you but I don't think she is up to it," Dad adds. "Though she has recovered much faster since you've been here."

Can a meal last for three hours? Yes. If you have a lifetime of things to talk about. He wants to hear all about me getting stitches in my arm in kindergarten and the blueberry pie at Slice of Muse, my grandparents, my violin, and my friends. He tells me about his years in Dallas. The conversation is spectacular but I miss Mom and wish she were at this table with us.

"Abby, I wish I had stayed in touch with your mom. I do. But I moved to Delhi with a new job and then films happened to me. I was thrown into the deep end of the pool. Fame is not easy to deal with. And before I knew it, years had flown by. I did think about trying to contact her but I thought she was probably married and had a husband, kids, job…"

He trails off. What would have happened if Dad had picked up the phone and called her? How would my life have been different?

I guess we'll never know.

His voice takes me out of my thoughts. "You and Shiva are becoming friends he tells me."

"We are. Did you know Shiva makes rotis and we feed the dogs in our neighborhood?"

Dad takes a sip of his coffee and signals for the check. "One day we will do more. We'll build a place to help animals and call it Abby's Place."

Is it another promise of tomorrow?

On the way out, we stop at the gift shop. Wow! The choices. I wasn't going to buy anything; but, finally, on Dad's insistence I choose presents for everyone back home—mugs, table mats, scarves, pottery, and a kurta—a tunic shirt—for Grandpa. I leave the gift shop with more bags than I can carry.

While driving home, Dad stops the car on Marine Drive. He motions out the window. "These lights are called the

Queen's Necklace, Abby. I loved coming here with my father when I was little."

The lights look like diamonds on a choker, encircling the pitch-black ocean. I hug the thought that he's shared them with me.

❧ CHAPTER 17 ❧
DHAK DHAK DHIN

What do you wear when you visit a movie studio and there's a cute boy involved? I have no idea. I try on several outfits. Jeans with blue-striped T-shirt, jeans with a tank and crocheted vest, capris with the striped T-shirt, white Bermudas with black top, two skirts, and a sundress. Or almost the entire contents of my suitcase.

What look am I going for? Casual, cute, or sophisticated? I don't know. Am I trying to impress Shaan? Am I trying to make Dad proud? Could one outfit do both? I need a stylist or at least a good fashion magazine to copy from. Finally, I choose the skinny jeans with the red tank and swirly crocheted vest.

Dad left a few hours ago. He has to do some publicity shots and asked us to come around eleven. "So you don't get bored waiting around," he'd said.

I don't know why he's so worried about us being bored. We're going to be on a movie set!

Shiva drives Shaan and me to Film Studios. "I love song shooting," he'd declared that morning as he rushed around finishing up all his morning duties.

Shaan whispers, "I hope you weren't too freaked by our rickshaw-bike chase. I should've known better."

Shiva looks back at us suspiciously.

"No, no. I mean, I didn't have time to think about it," I whisper.

"Jay's okay—a bit crazy at times," Shaan says.

I roll my eyes, not entirely sure of Jay's sanity.

Shaan points to a poster of shirtless Dad and snickers. "Hey, weren't you going to paint shirts on him?"

A woman in the car next to us pokes half her body out her window and takes a picture of the poster.

Shame on her! I turn as red as a summer strawberry.

Shaan finds it hysterical. He grabs my camera and takes a picture too. "To show your friends," he laughs.

"Shut up!"

Our car slows at the gates to the studio. There is a small group of people at the entrance hoping to catch a glimpse of the stars entering the compound.

"Our car is obviously a disappointment. No film stars here." Shaan shrugs his shoulders at the crowd and silently mouths sorry.

I don't know what I expected but the set is a stunner. The production team has recreated the interior of a nightclub. I've never been inside a nightclub, but that's how they look on TV and in the movies—dark, smoky, cave-like, forbidden.

Shaan and I stand with our mouths gaping. Loud music echoes and literally shakes the set. A zillion people scurry around. Huge lights are pushed and rolled into place. White reflector screens are being positioned and argued about. The catering staff scampers around loading snacks and water on long tables. Production crew members yell out in Hinglish to one another across the set. It's as busy as ants at a picnic.

The nightclub set is like a stage. In a theater, beyond the stage, is the audience. On a movie set, there are wires, blazing lights, and the crew. Outside the stage lies the junky reality of rafters and exposed two-by-fours, ropes, hammers, and nails. A dozen dancers with dramatically kohled eyes are already in place. The energy bounces off the crew like magnets. I have goose bumps.

A woman shouts orders in a booming, naturally forceful voice. She obviously doesn't need a bullhorn. Comfortably plump but not overweight, she wears a long white tunic over harem pants. She has tied her blue *dupatta* efficiently around her waist. Her hair is yanked back into a no-nonsense braid.

She has a leather strap of bells around her right foot and she keeps a beat. "*Ek, do, teen, char*," she chants.

"One, two, three, four," Shaan translates.

"*Dhak, dhak, dhin, dhin.*" She sings along with the song that fills the room. The music is loud enough to drive every other thought from my mind. The dancers wear satin skirts that sit lower than any low-rise jeans I've ever worn. Their shirts ended just below their boobs so their sculpted midriffs are bare.

Dancing with the Stars meets *Arabian Nights* in Bollywood.

"Stop the music, *yaar*! All of you," says the dance director, making a sweeping movement toward the dancers. "Move those bellies. Move them as if they have a life of their own and are separate from you. Have you seen a belly dancer move? Let's try it again. We don't have all day. One, Two, Three, Four."

As the dancers move, their bellies disconnect and become hula-hoops.

Watching the dancers contort their hips makes me giggle helplessly. Shaan pinches me. "Abby, stop! They'll throw us out."

"I know," I manage to sputter, "But I can't—" Another wave of giggles drowns me. Sometimes once I start, I can't stop. Honestly!

Shaan stifles a smile as he looks at me. "Abby! Shut up!"

The dance director gives me a withering look that takes me straight back to second grade.

I stop giggling. I whisper to Shaan, "She reminds me of my second-grade teacher, Miss Glen. She would glare at me when I sharpened my pencils too long."

Shaan says, "Okay, since we don't know her name, let's name her Miss Glen for the day."

I let out a quick giggle before Miss Glen can see me.

Dad walks onto the set minutes after Shaan and I find a corner tucked away in the shadows near the fan. He looks around for me and calls, "Abby, where are you?"

I leap up and Shaan follows.

"Hi, you two! Today's song has Rani and me. In the first shot, I woo Rani, who is participating in a dance off at her local nightclub."

"Then you both sing the song with different backdrops to show different times and the relationship developing," finishes Shaan with a grin.

"You know Bollywood movies!" Dad smiles. "Do you like the song?"

Shaan hums *Dhak, dhak, dhin, dhin* to the music.

Dad laughs. "That's it! It's catchy."

"It's like an earworm," says Shaan. "I have to sing it."

Dad and Shaan hum together. I want to join in but I'm

too conscious of making a fool of myself. The string quartet jumps in and plays *dhak dhak dhin.*

Miss Glen calls out to Dad, "Naveen, *yaar*, Rani's not here yet but why don't we try the sequence of steps?"

"I'll be right there," Dad calls back. "Abby, Salima is around, so let her know if you need anything. Remember to drink bottled water only," he says, pointing his index finger at me.

"I'll remember," I say.

"He sounds like a parent," Shaan says, looking at me with a strange expression. "Like my mom."

Can a heart sing while it's sinking? He's my dad and he cares about my well-being. I'm thrilled. But after my talk with Dad last night, I'm terrified that our secret will be revealed too soon. I like my anonymity. I'm sure Shaan would never spill the beans but if he noticed Dad's parental tone, maybe someone else would too. I have to warn Dad to watch his behavior. I'm on his side and now we were a team.

"He's repeating my mom's instructions," I lie.

"So tell me," Shaan says, "how exactly do you know Naveen Kumar?"

My heart definitely stops singing. Thankfully, I don't have to answer the question because someone cranks the volume up on the music, which distracts Shaan. Dad's taken his place with the dancers and they rehearse. *Dhak, dhak, dhin, dhin.*

Dad has an energy and rhythm that is amazing. I guess I should've known that from the video and the movie I've seen, but in person is different. Where and when did he learn to dance like that? Dad leads the group as they strut and boogie to the booming music.

Shaan and I watch. Miss Glen joins Dad on stage. They discuss and mark spots with chalk then turn and twirl and count steps.

Shaan leans in. "So, do you want your Hindi lesson for the day?"

"Yes, yes, I do." I grin. "What does *yaar* mean? I hear it all the time."

"Oh, it means friend. It's slang like 'man.' Abby, *yaar*, you got that?"

"Shaan, *yaar*, what's the next word?" I laugh.

"So *dhak, dhak* is the sound of the heart beating. Kind of like saying, my heart beats boom, boom." Shaan taps his hand on his heart to mimic a beating heart.

"And what's *dhin, dhin*? The sound of the beating drum?"

"You got it," Shaan answers.

We sing the opening bars together. Shaan makes exaggerated gestures and generally clowns around. His sense of humor is infectious and I'm cracking up the whole time. I hate the thought of not seeing him when I go home.

Just then, Rani glides in.

"Did you know Rani means queen?" Shaan whispers.

I didn't know that. She definitely looks regal. It's my first glimpse of her. Jeez, her name fits her like a glove. She wears a fitted, cleavage-revealing top with mirrors sewn on it. It has strings tied across the back as if the tailor had run out of fabric and this was the only way he could think of to hold the fabric together. It shows a generous hunk of midriff. Her red skirt swings to the floor. Her face is slathered in makeup for the camera. She doesn't need it. She's obviously beautiful.

A woman shuffles behind her with a bottle of water. A man holds an umbrella over her to prevent the cruel sun from damaging Rani's flawless skin on the two-minute walk from her trailer. Another woman holds her skirt so the train-like hem won't touch the floor.

OMG.

"What a diva!" I whisper to Shaan.

"Serious hottie alert," he whispers back.

She saunters up to Dad and Miss Glen and air kisses them both. Dad calls Shaan and me over and introduces us. Rani air kisses me and says, "I'm looking forward to getting to know you, sweetie."

I politely say, "Thank you. Same here."

I wondered if she knows I'm Naveen Kumar's daughter. How close are they?

"Okay, back to work," Miss Glen says, taking charge. "We

are behind schedule, *yaar*. I want to wrap this song in four days. Turn up the music. Everyone in place. Let's rehearse the opening moves."

No time for niceties with her. She's the real Miss Glen's twin separated at birth and raised halfway around the world.

Rani stands facing the wall at the back of the stage and sways. She thrusts her hip out and places her hand on it. The crisscross pattern of the strings weaves against her back. She lazily stretches her arms over her head and knocks her hip out some more. More than a dozen glass bracelets adorn each of her arms. She looks over her shoulder and snakes her hips to the music.

Wowza! Shaan and I gulp like goldfish for air. Grandpa Spencer would've said holy guacamole!

Dad then leaps behind her, kind of like he how he leaped off the screen on International Day a lifetime ago. He runs his fingers s-l-o-w-l-y down Rani's back and traces along the zigzag strings, then he flips her around and they gaze into each other's eyes.

Yech! Double yech! Barf bag, please.

"Let's try that again!" says Miss Glen. "Naveen, slow down the finger action, flip Rani around faster, and Rani, give him a smoldering look after. Burn him, *yaar*!"

I close my eyes in utter embarrassment and die a premature teenage death. I groan. "Oh Schmit!"

Shaan grins ear to ear. Annoyed because he's enjoying this and because I'm not, I do the mature thing and kick him. Hard.

"Why would you do that?" Shaan hops around and rubs his shin.

"This is too embarrassing!"

"Why? It's a song for crying out loud. Like a music video. It's a Naveen Kumar movie. You saw one the other day."

"I know," I say. "But it's different watching them in person."

"I don't get it. Why are you all embarrassed?"

I stare at him and try to move my facial muscles into a poker face. C'mon, Abby, you've done this before. My poker face is my triumph. First, I relax all facial muscles, even the ones that on the sides of my eyes. I make sure my eyebrows aren't lifted, scrunched, or arched. Oh, and my eyes, they should be blank but not in a duh-I-don't-get-it way but in a non-committal, oh-that's-interesting way.

My face won't listen to my brain. I want to scream and ask him, how would he like to watch his Dad romance some sizzling hot actress like Rani all afternoon? Of course, I can't.

❧ CHAPTER 18 ❧
BOLLYWOOD SHUFFLE

"You're crazy, you know. Of course I'm not embarrassed," I lie.

"Whatever, calm down. Forget I said anything." Shaan kicks the floor and walks over to the food table to get a packet of potato chips. "You want some?"

I decline. All I could think of is that I do not want to spill the beans. Seriously, what is wrong with me? I lost it over a song and dance! It's not as if someone is torturing me to extract my secrets.

After that, we're quiet. Awkward.

When the dancers have repeated the same movement fifty-three times, Miss Glen calls for a break. Rani needs to have her skirt adjusted. The director thinks the floor length doesn't look attractive and is hampering her dance movements. He probably wants to see more leg! The costume designer assures them the alterations will take fifteen minutes. Rani walks back to her gigantic trailer cave. Dad comes over to us. "You okay, Abby?" he asks.

"I'm fine!" I manage.

"Where and how did you learn to dance like that, Mr. K.?" Shaan asks and offers his packet of chips.

Dad takes a couple. He points to Miss Glen. "Once I knew I wanted to act in films, I went to her for dance lessons. I learned from the best. Till then I had no idea that hip joints were separate parts of your body like bellies," he says with a twinkle in his eye. "My costume is ready. I have to change. See you later," he calls as he walks away.

Shaan is searching in his chip bag. He takes out two huge chips and places them between his lips to form duck lips.

"Abby," his voice is muffled, "want to dance?"

How do you stay annoyed at someone with chip lips? I laugh. He changed the mood with his silliness.

"C'mon, *yaar!*" Shaan the duck offers his hand.

I seize two chips from the bag and join Shaan. We both talk through our duck lips. Shaan grins, losing his chips, and points to something behind me. I turned to see Dad walking from his trailer wearing an electric blue shirt and black pants. A costume for sure.

The molded satin of Dad's shirt highlights his stomach

muscles. The first three buttons are undone and—is that a medallion on a chain around his neck? He looks totally ready to be on *Dancing with the Stars.*

I burst into laughter. Dad grins wryly. "Glad you find it funny, Abby."

"Wow! Look at those abs." Shaan smiles.

Why this fascination with a set of muscles?

Miss Glen's voice booms, "Places."

All the backup dancers run into place. Rani returns. Her skirt now swings around her knees. She sashays back to her spot against the wall. Dad walks over and they are talking and laughing. So, she's gorgeous and funny?

Ms. Glen yells out, "One, two, three, *ek, do, teen.*"

The music blares. They've rehearsed enough by this time that Dad, Rani, and all the dancers get the sequence.

The director yells cut, and Miss Glen shouts, "Good job!"

That piece of the song would last for a minute or less on the screen, but it's taken hours to shoot. Wow, at this rate the entire song could take a week. Now I understand why the director and the choreographer stressed that the song have to be done in four days. They better hurry up.

After the shot, Dad retires to his trailer for a meeting. Shaan and I sit around forever watching the crew get ready for the next shot. They roll out the nightclub set and roll in the next one. It has the Taj Mahal as a backdrop.

Shaan decides we can kill time with a Hindi lesson. "I can't be your translator forever, you know, Abby. But here's another lesson. *Mera naam Abby Spencer hai* means my name is Abby Spencer."

I dutifully repeat and then find paper and a pencil and write the sentence down.

"What's your middle name?"

"Tara, after my dad's mother."

Shaan gives me a strange look. "My mom calls Naveen Kumar's mom Tara Aunty."

The silence roars and the quartet bows furiously. Oh Schmidt. My guard was down and I let what I thought was an innocent piece of information slip. I groan inwardly.

He lets the words lie there between us like a ball lobbed in my court.

Do I want to hit the ball back? I have a decision to make. Can I trust Shaan? I know that he's stumbled onto my secret. All I need to do is say yes. Unlike Priya and Zoey who are eight thousand miles away, Shaan is here. He could be someone to talk to about all of this.

But what about my promise to Dad? What if this leaks out in the wrong manner, hurts Dad's career, and ruins Mom's private life?

Shaan taps my knee. "*Tum, chup kyon ho?*" he asks. Then translates, "Why are you silent?"

My eyes beg for understanding. "Because I'm thinking. Because I'm scared. Because I really want to tell you my secret and I really don't. I'm so confused."

"Hey, relax. It's not a big deal."

I take a deep breath. "It's embarrassing to watch my dad trace zigzag lines on some glamour babe's bare back," I say, drawing out each word confirming his suspicion without saying the words.

Shaan's eyes pop. "Wow! You're joking, right?"

"It's true." There, I said it. My mouth is dry, but my shoulders slump in relief.

"There's something about the way he is with you. Like a father." Shaan spreads his hands out helplessly.

"Do you think others have noticed too?"

Shaan thinks about it. Then he looks me in the eye and says, "No."

"What makes you so sure?"

"I don't think anyone else watches you as closely," he mumbles. I can barely hear him, but I heard the words.

I feel a monumental blush creeping over my face. I'm as red as Rani's skirt.

Where should I look? What should I do with my hands and feet? I'm thrilled and overwhelmed.

A new bag of chips lie near Shaan. I fish for the two

largest chips and mumble through my chapped duck chip lips, "Thank you, Shaan."

Am I saying thank you for him noticing me or for assuring me that others haven't noticed or both?

"I know we can't talk right now with so many people around but call me tonight," I say.

"Sure. You know you can trust me with your secret. We can sign a contract in blood if you like," he teases.

"I'll take friendship bracelets instead please."

We're distracted by Miss Glen yelling at one of the production men. "I need more extras. Touristy-looking extras. This shot is in front of the Taj."

She spies us. "You two!" she calls out. "You would be the perfect tourists."

I guess it's pretty obvious I'm a foreigner to her. Then she says, "One *phirang*-foriegner to boot! Line up for make up."

She does not ask us. She orders us.

Shaan and I stand up. We're programmed to respond to adult orders.

"Oh my God! She's crazy, Shaan. We're not extras," I whisper urgently.

"I know. She's nuts but imagine how awesome it would be to be in a Bollywood movie for two seconds."

"No way! I can't dance like that," I protest.

Shaan tries to convince me. "They'll teach us. We're

supposed to be tourists, not dancers. We'll be in a crowd. We'll probably never show up in the movie."

"I don't know, Shaan," I waver. A not-so-little voice in my head says, *It would be cool to be in a movie for even one second. Especially one that stars Dad!*

Dad comes out of his meeting and walks over. Miss Glen intercepts him. "Naveen, I need these two kids as extras. I don't have enough and they would make perfect tourists."

Dad looks at us, "Sure, but it's their decision to make."

Shaan grins. "I'm in. Watch the birth of a star."

His attitude is infectious. How often will someone ask me to dance in a Bollywood movie? "I'm in too."

Game on! *Dhak, dhak, dhin, dhin!*

We stand in line with the other extras for makeup. I'm so nervous but Shaan keeps me laughing. He pretends to be interviewed by an imaginary reporter.

"I got my break as an extra in a Bollywood film," he replies to a pretend question.

Shaan assumes the imaginary reporter role with a water bottle microphone. "How do you feel on the eve of the premiere of the summer blockbuster?"

Shaan responds without the water bottle microphone, "Oh, it's amazing, *yaar*. What a journey it's been!"

I can feel my nervousness melting and I get into the spirit. How can I not when I'm around Shaan?

Dad and Rani lead the charge. Rani has changed and is now decked out like a glamorous rock chick, complete with a guitar, super tight T-shirt, and tattoo creeping up her lower back. She strides onto the set and tosses her wig. How many personas and costume changes would she have through this song?

We extras stand behind the front row of expert dancers. The steps are a bit like the Macarena, with a twist of the Texas two-step and a garnish of Bollywood enthusiasm. I learn to shake my hips. A skill I'll use back home, I'm sure—if only to hula-hoop!

I start out stiff and conscious but then see Shaan get into the mood with gusto. I can't let my dad down; I'm his daughter after all. I try to move my belly as ordered and almost throw out my back.

Dhak-dhak, shake-shake, *dhin-dhin*, spin—and bump into Shaan's head. Ouch! His head feels like a block of concrete.

We do the moves repeatedly until we get them right.

We dance until my mouth hurts from smiling and my feet blister. It's a day of excitement!

Dhak, dhak, dhin, dhin. The song from the movie shoot has embedded itself into my brain. What's the cure for a perfect earworm?

I play the tune on my violin that night and bask in the

admiration from Shiva, Dad, and Grandma Tara. They smile, rock, and clap, and I get into my groove, improvise, bow, and trill.

"More! More!" they cry when I stop.

So I play some more.

❧ CHAPTER 19 ❧
BUILDING BRIDGES

Grandma Tara and I turn the pages of my photo album for the third time. She obviously can't get enough of my baby pictures. It's as if she's studying my every moment as a child.

"In this picture, you look like Naveen," she says, pointing to a picture of me sitting on the floor with mashed bananas all over my face.

I'm probably a year old in that picture.

"You think so?" I ask skeptically.

"Yes," Grandma Tara says. She asks Shiva to get a picture from her room. He comes back with one of my father's baby pictures as proof. There is a distinct resemblance, the grin, the chin, the way we both embrace the camera.

Mom should see this! "Can I have this picture?" I ask.

"Of course you can have the picture. I wish I could

have cleaned your face after that banana feast," she says wistfully.

I squeeze her hand. I would've liked that too.

"Abby, I'm getting stronger again and I want to search through my husband's old papers and see if I can find anything. I vaguely remember him telling me that one of Naveen's American friends had called. Naveen was in Delhi then for his job."

My heart flutters.

Grandma Tara looks through me as if she's looking at her past. "I told Naveen this yesterday. So many of us have lost our children to America. My husband was afraid that Naveen would go back too. But I don't think he would have ever kept the news of a child from Naveen. Not his own flesh and blood. He valued family too much. I have to believe that. If he read your mother's letter and knew about you but still decided not to tell Naveen or me, it would break my heart, *beta.*" Her eyes shimmer.

I don't know what to say so instead I lean on her shoulder.

"Your mother says she is sure the letter was received?"

"Yes, she registered it," I explain.

After that, Grandma Tara and I don't say anything. We don't have to. Instead she brushes my hair till it shines.

I want Mom to know Dad again, today's Dad. I want her to be friends with Grandma Tara and Shiva. On any

166

given day and moment, I alternate between anger at how things worked out and trying to accept that none of us could change the past.

I talked to Shaan about it last night when we were returning from the movie studio. Now that he knows my secret, it's nice to share honestly.

"It sucks that you didn't have your dad growing up," said Shaan. "But what you can do? It's the past."

I laughed. "You have a point."

Shaan's practical advice burst my whiny self-pitying mood.

"Hey, could you write a song about it?" Shaan suggested with a smile.

"I ain't got no daddy?" I sang in a jazzy blues wail. "No, Shaan, I don't write songs. I could play a violin piece."

"You should do that!" Then he turns serious. "You know how they say live in the moment and stuff?" Shaan was trying to be helpful. "Like I know I can't change the fact that I didn't play baseball as a kid, but I can play now if I want to."

"So you're saying focus on getting to know Dad today?" I asked.

"Yup!" Then he changed the subject. "Hey, watch this hilarious clip on YouTube of a baby who's scared of his own mom when she sneezes." Once again, Shaan has lightened my mood and made me smile.

A few days ago, I said to Shiva, "I wish I'd known you all my life." He clucked at me, wagging his finger. "No change life. You friend now."

I guess Shaan and Shiva both agreed to not regret the past.

It feels weird though to have these two sides of my family who haven't met each other. Like the two banks of a river and I'm the bridge. They're all a part of me. Why can't they be part of each other?

Two cultures. Two countries. Two Abbys? No. I'm still one, thank God. So I come up with the next best solution. Technology. I decide I'll introduce Mom and Grandma Tara over Skype.

Grandma Tara is reluctant when I suggest the meeting. "I don't like that thing," she says, gesturing to the computer.

I plead and Grandma Tara melts.

Mom is hesitant too. "Abby, are you sure your grandmother is up to it?"

"She is, Mom. And we can keep the call short, I promise."

I set up the computer in the family room and drag Grandma Tara to the table and sit her down. She keeps adjusting and fiddling with her sari.

I log in and say hi to Mom. Her brow is creased.

Now that we're all together, talk about awkward. Well, at first it's Skype's fault. We don't have the best connection. I try to compensate for the awkwardness by being as perky as a morning talk show host.

They both walk on eggshells that I can hear crunch each time they speak. The string quartet plucks strings gingerly like they're playing an Asian folk song.

"Mrs. Kumar, it's so nice to see that you are recovering. I hope having Abby over has not been stressful for you." Mom is courteous, like she's talking to some business acquaintance.

"Oh, no, no! How could it? Abby has helped me to get better. Having her here is God's blessing." Grandma Tara hugs me. "Meredith, maybe one day you will come?" asks Grandma Tara. "I would like to meet you."

"Oh! That would be wonderful. I've never visited India," Mom answers.

I jump in and hijack the conversation. "Mom, I visited Dad's movie set yesterday. He was shooting a song with this actress named Rani." Grandma Tara half smiles. "Anyway, you'll never believe this, but Shaan and I were extras in the song."

Mom gasps. "Excuse me?"

And I prattle on and tell her all about Miss Glen and the Taj Mahal set and the makeup and dancing till my feet were sore.

"Slow down, Abby. Settle down," Mom laughs. "I can't follow you."

Grandma Tara jumps in, "It is so nice to have a young person in the house. Meredith, thank you for letting her come. I will talk to you again soon. I'll let you and Abby talk." Then she slowly stands up and shuffles out of the room.

"Okay, so Shaan and I probably won't make it in the final movie. We'll likely end up on the cutting room floor, but it was soooo fun."

"Oh, Abby, this movie stuff is crazy. Have you told Priya or Zoey? Honey, you're halfway through your stay already. I'm glad you're not homesick."

I wish I can tell her that at times I am, but I don't want her to worry. Like the moment during the motorbike chase or when I felt helpless seeing the slums. Sometimes, when I struggle to communicate with Shiva or when I suddenly want a burger and fries.

But I don't tell her any of that. There isn't time.

Dad asks to talk to Mom, and they exchange pleasantries.

Then Dad is all business. "Meredith, I have a plan for releasing the info. Abby, don't leave. You need to hear this too."

Do I?

Dad tells her about the photo shoot and interview with *Film World* and reminds Mom that the media might try to find her.

"You know how much I hate that idea," Mom says.

"Naveen, I never imagined you'd be a celebrity. This was supposed to be a personal issue."

"Well, I'm a celebrity, Mere," Dad snaps. "I can't change that, and in today's world celebrities are not entitled to personal lives, and keeping Abby a secret forever is not an option, is it?"

Mom is silent and so am I. We both know Dad is right.

"Meredith, you are the mother of my child," Dad reminds her, an edge to his voice. "We need to get through this with as much dignity as we can and hope that the media loses interest. Let's make this as boring as possible."

"Naveen, you entered Abby's life yesterday, I have been there forever," Mom say with just as much edge as Dad.

"And are you suggesting that's my fault?"

Mom calms down a bit. "No, but you don't get to come in and make decisions."

"Meredith, I am only making decisions that you cannot make because you don't know my life or my circumstances. We have already talked about this."

Whoa! The tension in the room is human, like a fourth person. Everyone is trying to keep a tight leash on his or her emotions and the control feels nuclear. Like it could erupt and destroy us all. The string quartet screeches.

I jump in with both feet. Miss Perky to the rescue!

"Hey, Mom, I get to buy a new outfit for the photo shoot!"

No one even cracks a smile. I tried.

Then they say I can leave. I shut the door behind me. It stays shut for a while and I can hear their voices. They sound frustrated at first, but I think I hear a laugh or two at the end.

Shiva sees my face after the Skype session and knows I need a distraction.

I spend the afternoon with him learning to make *pooris*, a type of fried bread. Like if you fried biscuit dough. Yummy! Why haven't I eaten these at Bombay Palace in Houston? Grandma Tara watches.

Shiva rolls a perfect four-inch diameter circle of whole-wheat dough. He makes it look as simple as pouring a glass of juice. Then he tests the oil to see if it's hot enough and slides the *poori* in. Golden brown, it puffs up within seconds. He fries the other side and then serves it to me.

I wolf it before the second one is ready.

Grandma Tara laughs. "Your father ate *pooris* like you do. I would tell him the story of the *poori* that ran away to escape being eaten by the wolf."

"Like the gingerbread man!" I squeal. I explain the gingerbread man story and Grandma Tara and Shiva are enthralled.

Then I insist that I make the next *poori*. The darn dough does not want to be a circle. It looks like a misshapen blob with arms and legs sticking out in weird places. Not quite a *poori* or a gingerbread man. Shiva laughs till he cries and then gallantly fries up my blob. It tastes good even if it looked like a hexagon with curved sides.

"You try again tomorrow," he says.

The big interview is a day away. Tomorrow I'm shopping with Rani.

Yippee and gulp for both!

∂ CHAPTER 20 ∂
BLING

Dad gives me a cell phone to use when I'm out and about in Mumbai.

Shopping trip with Rani! I text Priya and Zoey as I wait for her to pick me up.

Get out! texts Priya.

R u having tea with the Queen after? texts Zoey.

"Rani's car is here," Shiva says and I give Grandma Tara a kiss and rush out. The driver opens the door for me.

I don't recognize the stranger who sits in the backseat. Maybe it's an assistant. I smile politely and she nods. She wears a dark blue head scarf that covers her forehead and big sunglasses. Her outfit looks like someone pitched a tent around her. She keeps looking in my direction. Is she staring at me? I can't see her eyes.

We drive in weird silence for a while. Where is Rani? Will I meet her at the store?

Then the woman in the tent shakes silently as if trying to muffle a laugh.

Then she snorts. Honk! Just like that. I swear. Honk.

I look at the driver but he seems unmoved.

Loud snort *again*. Too bizarre.

She reaches across the seat and touches my hand. I jump and she doubles over with laughter.

She takes off the sunglasses and continues to snort and laugh and sputter.

"Rani?" I ask. I couldn't have been more surprised at the deglamorized actress.

"I want to take you to an ice cream place without being recognized," she explains. "I do this all the time." She gestures to her outfit.

It broke the ice and in a weird way made her human. She isn't all royalty and air kisses. I like this Rani.

I take a picture of disguised Rani and me eating the creamiest mango ice cream ever. Rani is right, her disguise works.

Then we get down to business and go to Globatique. Once in the store, she takes off the caftan tent, head scarf, and glasses. She wears jeans and a T-shirt underneath and no makeup, but she's still beautiful. The salespeople recognize her and can't do enough to please her.

The clothes are exquisitely hand beaded and embroidered and probably have fairy dust sprinkled on them. I want to soak in the vivid, fabulous colors. The manager brags that they beaded a gown for the girlfriend of a Saudi Prince and shipped an evening bag for the Duchess of Snobville.

Whoa! Maybe this is the place for Rani to shop, but not for me.

I know Dad is paying but even so, these prices are crazy. I look at the tag of a top that catches my eye. Twelve thousand, five hundred rupees. One dollar is fifty-one rupees. I rounded it to fifty since dividing by fifty is easier. I've been dividing for the last hour and my head hurt. Two hundred and fifty dollars! I've never bought a single outfit for that much, not even when I was the flower girl in my aunt's wedding, let alone a piece of an outfit!

I clutch my purse as if it might shrivel in embarrassment and decide to flee.

"For you, very nice," says the sales guy.

I shake my head and peek at another tag and divide furiously.

He reluctantly puts the top away and suggests another outfit. Peek. Math. Decision.

"For you. Very, very beautiful."

"No for me," I mirror his speech. The string quartet finds it funny, oh so funny. Shut up!

"For you. This for you," he insists, holding up an outfit that would make me look like a decked-out Christmas tree.

I don't need to peek or divide.

"No for me," I say firmly.

Why am I talking like this? No idea.

The pile of outfits soon rivals Mount Everest. Who will fold all these clothes and put them back? I'm beginning to sweat in spite of the air-conditioning.

What am I supposed to do? I know Priya doesn't buy such expensive outfits because she doesn't go to fancy-schmancy designers catering to royalty. I can't show up to her birthday party in a dress fancier than hers, could I?

Then Rani takes over.

She picks a blue chiffon hand-beaded tunic with tiny pearls and white pants that look like tights. It's soft and beautiful.

"Try it on," she orders.

I try it on, parade, and twirl for Rani who claps and giggles.

The moment is magical and after that, there is no stopping me. Rani created a monster.

I try on outfits that are magnificent and sequined, brocade and silk, exotic and colorful, edged with tinkle bells and embroidered with mirrors, Western, Indian, and fusion. Ooh la la!

Will I ever forget this afternoon? Not likely!

I bask in Rani's compliments. For a minute I feel like I belong there shopping with her.

In the end, I choose a relatively simple lavender sheathlike tunic for the photo shoot. It's perfection. It has understated embroidery in a yoke around the raised mandarin collar and pants to match that look like tights. It's a *churidhar*, or tights, and kurta, a tunic, I'm told.

Rani approves. I almost pass out looking at the price tag.

A white strapless silk dress with red poppies bursting at the hem whispers to me. *Abby*, it says, *you could wear me again and again.*

It would be perfect for the red carpet opening of Dad's film.

Rani must've seen me staring. "Naveen asked me to make sure you picked more than one thing," she says.

I point to the dress and whisper, "The red would match the red carpet."

"We'll take that one too," Rani says to the sales guy and winks at me.

Woot!

The whole city is excited about the upcoming premiere night. Even Grandma Tara plans to come. She showed me the blue chiffon sari she would wear.

Before we leave, Rani puts her disguise back on. I clutch

my full shopping bags and feel like the shopanista. I need to watch myself or I might strut like one.

On the way back we stop to watch a game of cricket at one of the parks. "Shaan's learning to play cricket," I tell Rani.

Rani rolls her eyes and says, "Your dad lives for the game too."

"You know?" I ask surprised.

I've been wondering about their relationship. How close are they?

"Yes, he told me. Naveen and I have been dating for almost two years, so he trusts me. Don't worry, I can keep a secret," Rani assures me.

Two years is a while. I wonder if they plan to marry.

As if she can read my mind, she says, "We're committed to each other for now. Who knows what the future holds?"

I'm beginning to like Rani's honesty. When she drops me off at home, she says, "I'll see you at the premiere, Abby. Looking forward to it. And good luck with your interview."

That evening Dad and I sit with our feet stretched on the coffee table in the living room. I tell him I had a great day with Rani. He seems pleased. "So are you two getting married?" I ask to get his take on it.

He thinks for a moment. "We are dating," he says. "I like her. We haven't talked marriage."

The large windows look out over the ocean. The sun slowly inches toward the horizon. I will miss these sunsets. Some days you can even feel the fine mist in this room.

We have our photo shoot outfits. I wish the rest of this will be as easy. I can tell Dad is jumpy about tomorrow's interview with *Film World* too. It's going to be at a brand-new hotel near the airport. The editor feels it will make a great setting for the pictures. "What do you think she'll want to know?" I ask Dad.

"She'll probably want to know a few things about you. She'll ask about your experience being in India and our relationship, I think." Dad rubs his chin. I've noticed he does that when he's stressed.

"I really don't know though," Dad mumbles.

"What if she asks why Mom didn't tell you sooner?" My voice is soft as I struggle to keep the fear out of my voice.

Dad rubs his chin again. "Abby, if she asks those types of questions, leave them to me. Don't answer anything you don't want to. In fact, I would prefer that you don't tackle those types of issues. It is her job to dig for a sensational story that can sell magazines. I know how to deal with that. Remember, my staff has vetted her. They think she'll be soft on me because we have been friends and she needs the magazine sales that a breaking story with me on the cover will bring."

I nod, relieved.

We stare at the rhythm of the waves. The crimson sun finally dips under the water. I can imagine the fish under the sea saying, "Hey, sun, you're home."

Grandma Tara is saying her evening prayers in the next room. She rings her small silver bell and I go and sit by her. She's lit jasmine incense sticks as she does each evening. With a twinkle in her eye, she tells me, "I ring the bell to make sure God is awake and listening to me."

Then she closes her eyes and prays, her hands together in a namaste. A few minutes later, she looks at me and says, "I pray for you both. Krishna will take care of you."

Dad yells out from other room, "Is that a promise?"

I go back to the living room and Grandma Tara shuffles off to her room. She returns moments later with a tiny box in her hands that she hands to me. "Abby, these were mine when I was a girl. I want you to wear them tomorrow and maybe to the premiere and to keep them if you like them."

Overwhelmed, I stare at the little box in my hand.

"Open it, Abby." Dad nudges me.

I open the box. On a bed of royal blue velvet lie the most beautiful tiny drop pearl earrings. My gut feels happy. Grandma Tara wants to give me heirloom earrings!

"If you don't like them, I will buy you something new that you like," Grandma Tara hurriedly says.

I'm dumbstruck. "No, no. Wow! Grandma Tara, I'll wear them tomorrow, but I can't keep them. They're too beautiful."

"I insist," says Grandma Tara. "I have to pass them down to the next generation. And you are my granddaughter."

Grandma Tara sees me as the next generation. Granted Dad isn't married and doesn't have other kids, but he will for sure. She truly considers me her own. Someone to protect her legacy.

I give her a tight hug. "One day, I will pass them on too."

Dad has been a silent smiling spectator. Now he says, "Abby, don't lose them or she'll be hopping mad."

Horrified, I look at them both. "I would never, ever, ever lose them."

Then I realize that Dad is joking! Somehow, we all feel better.

Dad stretches. "Okay, Abby. I have to get back to work."

I go to my bedroom, lay out my outfit on the bed, take a picture, and post it.

Check it out! I write. I get a bunch of likes in minutes.

The next morning, Thomas and Salima prep me for the interview as we drive to the hotel. Dad will meet us there.

Salima asks, "Are you nervous? Don't be." Easy for her to say.

Thomas hands me a list of dos and don'ts. Seriously? If

this list is supposed to help and make me calm, it doesn't. Then they go over the list with me.

Greet her with a namaste. Okay.

Think before I answer anything. Don't answer anything you don't want to. Could I run?

Don't volunteer extra information about your mom. Not likely to.

Pretend it's not a big deal. Really?

Don't say anything negative about India. As if I would!

Don't let your guard down and chat. Maya is good at making you feel like she's your best friend. Got it.

Do not say anything that suggests that you didn't know Naveen Kumar is your dad and a Bollywood star until recently. OMG!

Thomas's parting shot is "Don't let your dad down." I so didn't need that reminder.

My hands are clammy. We're almost there.

The hotel looms like a massive red stone fort transported from another time and place. The car pulls into the entrance. Red turbaned and uniformed security guards and hotel doormen leap to attention. The metal detectors at the entrance remind each person who walks in of the real threat of terrorism.

Dad arrives from the studio and meets me in the grand foyer.

The editor of *Film World*, Maya, sees us and waves. She wears a printed yellow cotton sari. Her black-rimmed glasses are perched on her head, the beaded strings dangle on either side of her face.

Dad and Maya shake hands. Then he introduces us. "Abby, meet Maya, an old friend from my television days."

"Naveen, I couldn't be more thrilled that you chose us to tell your story. Really. Especially with your new film, your first home production about to premiere. You must be so excited." She squeezes Dad's arm. She turns to me and says, "And you look gorgeous."

Then she gets down to business. "The lavender color of Abby's kurta will look stunning out in the courtyard. Naveen, we have some shirts laid out for you to choose from."

We step outside into the courtyard with the lattice wall with lush bougainvilleas and mosaic fountain gently spilling water. A photographer, his assistant, Dad's makeup and hair people, and Salima are already out there.

Salima whisks me away to hair and makeup. Ooh la la!

I'm in the land of glamour. I hum to myself as the hair stylist puts goop in my hair and sculpts it into beauty. Could this be any more different from school pictures with the mandatory marble blue-gray background and kids trying to cover their zits and tuck down their hair?

A small voice in my head asks, *But is this world real or fake?*

I touch my earrings from Grandma Tara, reassuring myself that they are real.

&CHAPTER 21&
ALMOST FAMOUS

Simon says look to your right.

Simon says chin up. Eyes down. Smile. Tilt toward Naveen.

I'm a smiling robot.

Thank goodness Dad is there. He's done hundreds of photo sessions.

He's a goofball and teases me until I relax and almost forget that we're posing for pictures. Dad even hoists me onto his shoulders. An hour later we're done. Maya says she'll go through the pictures and choose some for Dad's final approval.

"I'd like a picture for my desk," he says.

Woo-hoo! I'm out of the closet and on his desk. I borrow Dad's cell phone and call Shaan. "The photo shoot was all right and crazy and fun and weird," I tell him.

"Do I get a picture? Of you?"

I blush, glad the conversation is on the phone and he can't see me.

"Sure," I say, trying to act as if cute boys ask me for my picture every day.

"What's next?" he asks.

Huh? Oh! I'm still thinking about Shaan wanting my picture.

"The awful interview," I manage to say. "It feels worse than ten biology tests."

Dad, Maya, and I hunker down in one of the hotel's suites for the interview. An array of pastries and sandwiches sit on the table between us. You'd think it was a party.

Maya sits across from us. The sides are drawn.

She turns on her recorder and places it on the table. The red light blinks at us. My face feels flushed.

"Uh-oh!" says Dad trying to diffuse my nerves. "She's in reporter mode now."

Maya laughs and waves away Dad's comment. "Naveen, tell me about your years as a student in America. You've never talked of that time in your life to the press. What were they like? You obviously made some good friends." Maya's last comment has an edge as she stresses "good friends."

I reach for a piece of chocolate cake and a fork to give my hands something to do.

"They were carefree years. I was eighteen when I went abroad, a child." Dad leans back and sips his coffee. "I attended university in Dallas. It was a great campus. I'd never met so many different people. I soaked it in. Meredith and I met in my marketing class. I got to know and love America through my friends."

"You and Meredith were obviously good friends. Were there other good friends?" Maya's innuendos are making me want to slug her. Instead, I stab my cake.

"Tell us more about Meredith," Maya says.

I can tell that Dad isn't happy by the way he tightens his jaw, but he doesn't let it show. In a calm voice he says, "Meredith is the mother of my child and a wonderful person. But she is a private person, not a celebrity. She deserves her privacy."

Maya looks taken aback.

Go, Dad!

"When did you return to India?" Maya asks.

"I had such a good time that it took me five years to graduate. Back then, I dreamt of being a news anchor and I knew it was time to come home."

"What was your first job after you came back?"

"I got a job as a junior reporter in the news department in Delhi and moved there. You were a reporter too. Isn't that when we met? We were all broke and worked round the clock." He laughs. "I remember an invitation to your parents' house for dinner being a special treat."

Maya stretches and turns off the recorder and gets up to pour some tea. They laugh and reminisce about their time in Delhi. Dad's let down his guard and his feet are up on the coffee table. I lick the last smears of chocolate off my fork.

Maya returns and discreetly turns the recorder on again.

"Why have your fans not been introduced to Abby before? Where have you been hiding Abby?"

If you were a fish swimming along a lazy river, the question would a metal hook coming out of nowhere.

He didn't know I existed. How could he introduce me to his fans? I open my mouth and Dad shoots me a look that says *I'll handle this.*

"Abby…" he stops. "I," he starts over, "I wanted to let Abby have as normal a childhood as possible. I did not want the media involved in her life."

I gulp. He didn't tell the truth.

Dad rubs his chin. "I don't think the harsh glare of the media is appropriate for a child. Her mother raised Abby in Houston. It was easier for her to have a normal childhood."

Maya smiles. "Great decision. I wondered for a moment if you only recently met each other. Silly me!"

Each pore on my skin crawls. I set my plate on the table.

"Abby and I feel like we have been together forever," he says, looking at me.

Dad does not outright lie about how involved he's been in my life, but he answers the questions in a way that it seems like he's known me forever.

If he tells Maya that he didn't know about me until a few weeks ago, she'd ask why. Then she'd asked why Mom hid the fact from Dad and it would open a basket of drowsy snakes.

"We know each other better than many dads and daughters who live in the same house. And now that Abby's older, she plans to visit Mumbai often."

At that moment, I'm so glad I had the allergic reaction to coconut and it brought me to Mumbai.

"Does your mom plan to visit too?" Maya asks me.

"She'd love to visit India," I say truthfully.

"Abby, what was it like for you to not always have your dad around? Did you miss him?"

I latch onto the last part. I can answer that honestly. I'm terrified of lying and falling into a sinkhole of more lies.

"I always miss him when he isn't around."

"Have you met Rani?" Maya persists.

From the corner of my eye, I can see Dad's face tightening.

I am my dad's daughter. In a perky tone I gush, "Rani

is so beautiful. I saw her on the set of Dad's movie." And I babble on about being an extra in the song till Maya's eyes glaze over and she turns to Dad.

"How come you and Abby's mother didn't stay together?" Maya drops her fishhook again.

Dad swims around it. "C'mon Maya. It's in the past. I was twenty-two. Meredith was twenty-one. We were kids. We will always be together for Abby."

Way to go, Dad. I suddenly have a newfound respect for him.

"How do you think your fans will react to you having a teenage daughter?" Maya asks.

"My fans love my films. My personal life belongs to me. I hope they continue to support my films."

Maya tries to bait Dad a few more times but then she quits. She's suspicious but she realizes that Naveen Kumar has a story and he's sticking to it.

"I think I have all the information I need." Maya says, gathering her things. "I have to do my job."

I exhale.

Dad stands up and smooths his pants. "And you did a great job as always. Interview is done. Tell me, how are your kids?"

They switch back to being old friends.

"If I don't see you before you leave, have a safe trip back, Abby," Maya says as she walks out of the suite.

The minute Maya and her team walk out of the room, I jump up and dance around the room. It's over. I didn't screw up. Dad matches me step for step. High five!

I eat another piece of cake and skip all the way to the car.

❧CHAPTER 22❧
UH—OH

On the car ride home Dad seems distracted. He stares out the window.

"Abby," he says, "Maya is a friend. She knew there was more to this story. She tried, but not too hard out of respect for our friendship. Others may not be as respectful."

I know that but I don't want to hear it.

"Abby, I chose this life. With fame comes lack of privacy. It's part of the business. I can take the potshots. But, I don't want you or your mom to be dragged in." He sighs. "What a day it's been. I have the worst headache." He leans his head on the backrest and closes his eyes.

My fists are balled. I wish I could delete parts of my life story and rewrite it. Start it over. Not have Dad walk into the story in the middle like a secondary character. I want to rewrite and have him with me at Doughnuts for Dad in elementary school. I want to have him warn Mom of his allergy when I first start eating solid foods. "Mere, Abby might have my deathly allergy to coconut."

I stare out the window at the street without seeing. I feel frustration rise in me. I need a door to slam.

Dad's house looms ahead of us. The usual crowd at the gate is larger today because his new film is coming out in two days and there is buzz about it. Each bus in the city seems to have his and Rani's faces plastered on it. Dad and Rani dancing.

When we get home, Dad goes to his room to rest and deal with his headache. I decide to walk over to Shaan's place. "I'll be back in an hour," I promise Dad.

I need the fresh air and sympathetic ear.

The waves beat against the rocks, foaming and spitting as I walk along the road. The sky is overcast and the humidity feels like a wet towel dripping down my shirt.

The paparazzi are staked outside, constant like the groups of onlookers. They are milling around the hood of a car a few feet from the gate. All of them have their cameras slung around their necks. They are chatting, killing time, and lying in wait for their prey—Dad. When he steps out, they jostle and shove each other for the best spot and train their lenses on him.

I hear them talking about Dad, I can hear his name

between other Hindi words. "Naveen Kumar! Naveen Kumar!" My Hinglish isn't good enough to understand them completely. But I know they're cracking jokes and being crude at Dad's expense. I hear Rani's name too. One of them made scummy kissing noises.

I keep my head down, my fists clenched.

The photographer who made the mocking sounds spies me and saunters toward me. He signals me to wait and says something I don't understand.

He raises his voice and this time in English asks, "Miss, you are living there?" and gestures to the house.

I nod but keep walking.

He follows.

"Miss, where's Naveen Kumar? We are waiting all day."

I don't respond.

"Hey, miss, I'm talking to you!" he says. My reflexes are on alert.

"Is Naveen Kumar busy with Rani?" he asks, smirking. His leer, his lewd tone, his innuendos push me over the edge of self-restraint.

Ooh! I want to punch him. He doesn't know my dad, but he feels like he could be familiar with him. He acts as if Dad owes him something. As if it's Dad's job to pose for him!

"Stop following me!"

"Miss! Miss! Come on, where is Naveen? Hey, miss, I'm talking to you!"

I snap, "You need to leave me and my dad alone!"

The moment the words leave my mouth, I bite my tongue. I want to reel the words back, swallow them. But just like you can't turn back the hands of time, I realize I can't wipe out words that have been uttered.

I know the photographer heard because I see the spark of shock, surprise, and then glee in his eyes. He must have seen the look of regret and alarm in my eyes.

He stops in his tracks and grins ear to ear like he's won the lottery. He reaches for the camera slung around his neck, focuses his lens, and has the nerve to say, "Thank you, sweetie!" before he presses the button and takes my picture.

Click! Click! Click! Click!

I stand there helpless, knowing there's nothing I can do that won't make the situation worse. I can't grab his camera or throw a hissy fit. It would only provide him with more ammunition. I give him the most hateful look I can muster. He doesn't blink. Turning away, he hails a passing cab, eager to report his discovery, I'm sure. He gives me a mocking salute before the cab drives away, emitting toxic black fumes.

I stand on the sidewalk, red-faced, shaking in frustration. I have no one to blame except my big mouth.

Way to mess it up, Abby! What would that man do? Nothing good, I knew that.

I walk to Shaan's house in a daze. I've never felt such hatred in my life. I want to scream, punch something, and kick all at once.

The minute Shaan opens the door, he knows something is wrong.

"Hey," he says and examines my red face, my hunched shoulders.

I can't speak.

I follow him to the living room. Luckily, no one else seems to be around.

"What happened?" Shaan asks. "Was the interview that bad?"

The interview! It seems eons ago. All the effort Salima and Thomas had taken to coach me had come to nothing.

"Abby, did you screw up the interview?"

I still can't speak. How do I explain myself?

"I followed all the rules for the interview," I say, "but I screwed it up anyway."

Shaan looks puzzled.

"I told the reporter guy outside to leave my dad alone!" I say.

"What reporter? At the interview?" Shaan asks.

I need to start at the beginning for Shaan to understand my panic.

I take a deep breath.

Shaan realizes this is serious. He waits in silence for me to continue.

"The interview actually went well," I say. "Maya, the lady who interviewed us was sweet to me. I mean she tried to dig and stuff, but Dad handled her well. We had this great photo shoot, and this amazing dinner the other day, and we've been bonding. Dad and me."

My voice is now shaking.

Impatient, Shaan interrupts, "What did you do?"

I tell him about the photographers outside Dad's house and just spill it all. I gulp. "Shaan, it was the way he said it. As if he owned Dad. I felt protective and I told him to just leave my dad alone!"

"You what?" he asks. Then he says in a calmer, more hopeful voice, "Maybe he didn't hear you. Or maybe he didn't understand or put two and two together."

I shake my head. "He heard. He understood."

Shaan is silent for a minute. "Are you sure?"

I nod.

"Oh Schmidt!" he says. Shaan has borrowed my phrase.

"What do you think he'll do?" I start crying. "Shaan, I messed it up, didn't I?"

He doesn't say anything. What can he say? He gets me some tissues and we sit in miserable silence.

"Abby, you can't go home with red swollen eyes. Let's go for a ride to the beach, get some air. Maybe we can figure something out. We barely have a few days left," says Shaan.

He's right.

We stand on the curb outside Shaan's apartment for a taxi. It starts to drizzle. A rickshaw sputters to a halt in front of us. The driver pokes out his head, "Where do you want to go?" he asks in Hindi. I'm surprised I understand him.

I've been wanting to ride in a rickshaw but Dad had said, "I don't know, Abby. I prefer you didn't. Shiva can drive you in a car wherever you need to go."

Well, Shiva can't drive me now. He isn't here. Dad said he *preferred* I didn't ride in one. He didn't forbid it. Did he?

Shaan gets in. The drizzle turns into rain. I throw caution under the motorized three-wheeler and get in.

The driver revs the engine, and with a loud put-put-put, we're off.

⋟ CHAPTER 23 ⋞
BUMPY RIDE

The rickshaw looks like a large motorized bug on three wheels. It bounces and hits every one of the dozens of potholes on the road to the beach. The first one sends Shaan and me into midair like two moles that were whacked. Shaan being taller hit the metal rod on the ceiling and cusses like a rapper. I don't quite hit the roof, but it's a near miss and I look up at it.

Wow! Oh wow!

On the roof is a multicolored collage of calendar pictures of Laxmi, Ganesh, Krishna, Rama, and other Hindu deities I don't recognize.

Shaan says with a grin, "All the Hindu gods are watching over us." He folds his hands to pay his respects.

I'm not sure how to react, not wanting to say anything offensive.

Shaan solves the problem. "You can smile you know."

I let my imprisoned smile out but I also say a silent prayer. I need all the help I can get.

The rickshaw can't really pick up much speed on its little engine but it can weave. When Grandma Spencer taught me to knit she chanted, "Abby, needle in and needle out." The rickshaw does exactly that. In and out, in and out, between cars and around garbage piles at the highest speed it's capable of hitting. Zoom! Zoom! Bump! It's the little engine that could.

The rain picks up. The rickshaw doesn't have any doors. At the stoplight, the driver lowers the rubber flaps on the sides to shield us against the damp. It's as much protection as crossing your fingers when faced with a bear.

The driver also decorated the front of the cab with a wild array of tinsel garlands. More pictures of dead and living Indian legends like Gandhi and—wouldn't you know it— Naveen Kumar are plastered in the front. The string quartet plays *dhak, dhak, dhin, dhin.*

Shaan points to the picture. "Your dad's watching you too."

By this point, my fractured funny bone is healed. I smile and shrug. "Dad and the gods. Maybe the gods will help me out and cure my big mouth."

If this rickshaw ride were under different circumstances,

I would've had a blast. I would've videoed the inside to show all my friends. I would've posted this ride on YouTube.

We hit another pothole. This time it throws us right into each other's arms. Are Mumbai's potholes helping my love life? Is it an omen? The rubber flap waves and sprays water on us, and in spite of the circumstances, we laugh and untangle ourselves, but still sit close.

And then something crazy happens. Almost as crazy as finding out your father is a Bollywood star. Shaan reaches over and. Holds. My. Hand.

Warm.

Slightly larger than mine.

Real.

Nice.

Tingly.

A perfect envelope for my hand.

I smile and lace my fingers within his. They fit. He squeezes my hand to reassure me, and somehow I know that while I have to face the consequences of my action, I'm not alone.

Shaan doesn't let my hand go till we get there.

The rickshaw sputters to a stop. We can see the ocean ahead of us. The waves remind me to breathe. The rain has petered off. Shaan says it's unusual for rain in November anyway. There aren't many people around. It's a weekday and it's still early in the afternoon.

Shaan and I get out of the rickshaw and he pays. "It's going to be fine, Abby. Relax."

We take off our shoes and walk toward the beach. The ocean breeze whips my hair around.

Shaan looks at his watch. "Abby, did you realize it's Thursday today. Your mom is asleep right now, but when she wakes up it'll be Thanksgiving."

It's the biggest business day for Mom. She sells more pies today than on any other day in the year. The shop remains open until noon. I usually help Mom at the store. After closing, we head to Grandma's house for Thanksgiving dinner. What I would give to be digging into one of her pies instead of having to deal with the mess I've created? A little voice says, *But then you wouldn't be holding hands with Shaan, the cutest guy ever.*

A row of food stalls stands on the edge of the sand near the street. They have thatched roofs, sandy floors, and rough wooden benches and tables for seating. Some of them are grinding chutneys, getting ready for the evening customers. The smell would have normally made me hungry but not today. Why can't I be sitting here, eating roasted corn on the cob with Shaan and celebrating the successful interview?

I dig my foot into the sand. I stare down at the splinter rising from the weathered wood of the table. It didn't pierce my flesh but it might as well have.

203

All I could think of is tomorrow and ugliness. What would that hateful photographer do? The string quartet plays suspenseful music.

❧ CHAPTER 24 ❧
NOWHERE TO TURN

Shaan and I walk on the beach before heading home. I'm not ready to return yet. I don't have a plan. Is there anything I can do?

How do you tell your father that you ruined the opening of his big movie and opened him up for tabloid trash because you can't keep a secret? A slip of the tongue they say is a fault of the mind. I think this slip is because of a rude, horrible photographer.

How do you hope that he forgives you?

How do you not crumble, crawl into a crevice, or curl up? I say that aloud.

Shaan grins at me. "Abby, are you trying to be a poet and use that figure of speech thing with the same sound?"

"Alliteration?" I ask.

"Yeah, that." Shaan grins. "Are you being all dramatic and poetic?"

I know he's trying to cheer me up so I play along. I smack my hand to my brow. "To tell or not to tell, that is the question."

"Uh, Abby, it's not actually," Shaan says, his face dead serious. "You gotta tell. The question is how and when?"

"I'm just going to say it. I don't think there's any way to sugarcoat or glaze this pie."

I'm miserable and Shaan drapes his hand over my shoulder to comfort me, and then lets it linger longer. I smile and drown in his gorgeous brown eyes and briefly rest my head against his shoulder. The sand slides between my toes and sticks. A gust of wind blows my hair onto my face.

He tucks my hair behind my ears and then bends down toward my face.

Freaked, I turn my face. Slightly. The kiss lands just right of my lips. I've been watching too many Hindi films in Mumbai. Kissing is rare in Bollywood films. Instead, faces come close, close, and closer and then the camera swings to a tree or a fire. Love the fire! Is it a metaphor? Or as the hero comes in for the kiss, the heroine turns her face away like me, Abby Tara Spencer.

My face feels flushed. Shaan looks disappointed. I am too.

On the rickshaw ride home, we sit close to each other, our sandy legs touching.

Shaan drops me off outside Dad's house. I squeeze Shaan's hand. "Wish me luck," I say. He hugs me and I lean in to kiss Shaan's cheek as I say good-bye. This time Shaan turns and our lips brush. So light I'm not sure it happens. Was that a kiss?

He laughs and says, "Good luck, Abby."

The rickshaw sputters away, splashing a puddle of muddy reality on my pants. I drag my feet as if I have ten-ton shackles on. I can hear both phones ringing inside the house, shrill and piercing.

A grim-faced Shiva opens the door. "Abby, where you go?"

Oops. I told Dad I would be home in an hour. Three hours later, here I am.

I walk into Dad's office and find him with Thomas, Salima, and a third man who I don't recognize.

"Where were you?" Dad asks. "You said you would be back in an hour. I was worried sick."

"I'm sorry. I really am," I say. "I went to the beach with Shaan and lost track of the time. I need to talk to you alone."

Maybe it's the tremble in my voice or how pale I look, but Dad's voice softens. "What is it? You can tell me anything, *beta*."

The endearment nearly does me in. I try to swallow the lump in my throat.

Thomas glares at me as if I'm trouble spelled with a capital *T*.

"Everyone, please leave us alone," Dad says.

They all troop out and Dad turns to me, puzzled.

I'm dumbstruck. I can't find the words. I search for the best way to tell him, but my thoughts and feelings are jumbled like strings of Christmas lights. Where do I start unraveling them?

"Dad," I say in a strange choked voice before Thomas knocks and comes in again. "Sorry, excuse me, Naveen, but it is the TV anchor for NDTV. They're covering the premiere tomorrow. They need to talk to you. He called twice when you were in other meetings."

Dad looks at me. "Abby, I have to deal with this now. Can we talk later?"

I flee.

I sit in my room for an hour thinking how to tell him about the photographer, but my mind is blank.

I think about how for the past few days, Grandma Tara and Shiva have been emotional that I'm leaving soon. After I played the violin for them yesterday, Grandma Tara hugged me. "I was getting spoiled by your performances every evening. I will miss them." Her smile wavered.

Shiva said he would make paneer for me next week, then realized I won't be there and was all sad after that.

I want to see Mom, Grandma, and Grandpa Spencer, but at the same time, I don't want to leave my newfound family in Mumbai. I wish I could be in two places at the same time.

Maybe after the whole thing blows up in the newspapers they'll hate me and won't want to see me.

Twice that evening I go into Dad's study, but I can't find the words and we're interrupted. I try, but I feel like something within me shuts down. My mind races. I barely eat dinner. And then a thought flits through.

Maybe the photographer would take the picture and the story to the papers and they will refuse to print the stuff after all.

It could happen. Maybe they'd call Dad first to check the facts.

I latch onto that thought.

Shaan calls later in the evening. "What did your dad say?"

"I didn't tell him," I whisper. "Shaan, I don't know how to tell him."

He's silent.

I call Mom. It's Thanksgiving morning in Houston. She must have left for work early. I leave a crazy message telling her how I've ruined it all. When I hang up, I wish I didn't leave the message.

I call Priya and Zoey but neither of them answers.

I toss and turn all night. My thoughts are like knives, piercing and painful. I finally nod off around four in the morning so I ended up sleeping late.

⇘ CHAPTER 25 ⇙
TODAY'S HEADLINES

When I wake up the house is quiet except for the sounds from the kitchen and the faint murmur of running water from Grandma Tara's bathroom.

Maybe the story didn't make the newspapers after all. Maybe the story…I chant, willing it to be true.

I tiptoe downstairs, hoping against hope.

Every morning, all the newspapers are delivered to the house. Today, the magazines and newspapers scattered all over the coffee table look like bloody, inflamed wounds you don't want to see.

I pick one up and drop it as though it's burned my fingers.

Meet Superstar Naveen Kumar's Secret Daughter
[insert horrible picture of me]
Where's Mrs. Naveen?

I scan the rest of the papers like an addict.

It's a Girl! And She's Thirteen! In the accompanying cartoon, a stork drops a teenage me on Dad's doorstep.

Naveen's Love Child. Made In USA.

Born In the USA. Hidden In USA?

Has the Queen Met Her Stepdaughter To Be? with a grainy picture of Rani and me on the set.

No! They dragged Rani into the mess too.

Daughter In the Closet.

Abby In the Box. A cartoon of me jumping out of a box, startling Dad.

And then some get uglier.

Naveen's Wild Youth Results in Teen.

Naveen Kumar's Battle for Custody.

Whoa! Custody? Now that's a thought that never entered my mind. Would he? My life is with Mom in Houston. For a few minutes, the idea of Mom and Dad fighting over me paralyzes me with fear. Then sanity returns. It's garbage. Poison. Hot off the press.

Could my flight please be *now*?

The newspapers mock me. I sit on the couch and close my eyes to shut them out but instead they transform into Oompa Loompas and stomp around.

The phone rings. It's Mom. She's beside herself. "Abby, what happened? What did you ruin?"

I spill it all. I tell her about how I lost my cool when the photographer goaded me. I had stupidly wanted to protect Dad. I read her the headlines—even the custody one.

Mom is speechless. When she finds the words, she says, "Oh, Abby, honey, this is awful. How has your dad reacted to all this?"

"I couldn't tell him last night. He's not home right now. The premiere is in a few hours."

"Abby, it's all my fault. I shouldn't have let you go alone to a foreign country. What was I thinking?"

"Mom, stop," I interrupt. "If I'd only kept my lips sealed like you and Dad told me, none of this would've happened."

"Abby, if you weren't coming home in a few hours, I would take the next flight to Mumbai. I promise. What was that custody headline you just read to me?"

Then before I can say anything she says, "Naveen has never mentioned that word. It's the ugly newspapers."

I sigh in relief. After I hang up, I just stare like a zombie. Where is Dad? Where is everybody?

Shiva comes running in. "Abby, he's home."

When Dad walks in, I notice he hasn't shaved. His eyes look disappointed and his shoulders droop.

"Did you see all this ugliness?" he says, waving at the newspapers. "Abby, I am so sorry."

He shouldn't blame himself. He could yell and tell me I was an idiot.

Wait. Then I realize. None of the newspapers have named a source. He didn't know I'm responsible for the leak. For a minute, I'm tempted. Can I just keep silent?

No!

I can't. I did have to live with myself.

What if the truth emerges after I leave and I hadn't owned up? That would make the situation even worse.

My mouth is dry. Then the stubborn lump melts and mercifully turns into words. Through my constricted throat, I manage to say, "I'm so sorry, Dad."

I take a few blubbery, gaspy breaths and launch into my confession. "Yesterday, I accidentally told one of the photographers to leave my dad alone."

Dad looks confused.

I take a breath and continue. "I was mad at him and the way the photographers bother and stalk you all the time."

I can't look at his face. "The photographer kept yelling 'Miss! Miss!' in my face and wouldn't stop following me, so I snapped. He pounced on my words, realized I slipped up, and then took pictures of me."

Realization dawns on my father's face. I can tell he's at a loss for words. His eyes cloud over, and he clenches and unclenches his fist.

"Can you do something?" I ask, angry. "Sue them?"

Dad looks weary. "It's not worth it. I should have protected you more."

He probably regrets the day he invited me to Mumbai.

Grandma Tara stands outside the door. Her eyes tell me she heard it all.

Shiva thinks the world can't be trusted anymore. All anybody wants is money he says and spits into the big rubber plant. He earns a look from Grandma Tara who doesn't think the world has become so materialistic and unethical that Shiva should spit in the house.

"I'm sorry too, Grandma Tara," I tell her. "I've ruined everyone's plans. I know Dad was looking forward to talking about the first film he's produced."

Grandma Tara holds my hand. "This is not how I wanted this day to be. The premiere is in the evening. Then there is the big celebration dinner party and your flight leaves at two in the morning."

I wish I could board that plane this minute and literally fly away from the disaster I've created.

The phone continues to shrill.

Riiiiing.

Riiiiiiiing.

Drilling into my brain.

Making me cringe every time.

214

Dad stays holed up in his office, surrounded by his team. I slink in.

I cower seeing Dad read his email. "The damn rags jumped on the story," he says, pacing the room.

Thomas and the gang are silent.

"Nobody cares that I put my blood, sweat, and time into this movie," he says, his jaw clenched. Then he punches the wall with his fist.

If it had been drywall at home, he would have left a big gaping hole. But this is a concrete Mumbai wall. The sound of flesh pounding concrete sears into my brain. I bet it hurt.

I steal out of the room, terrified.

I mope around for hours doing nothing. Later, Shaan comes over to say good-bye. He looks at the newspaper-strewn table and sighs. "Abby, it will all work out."

I nod. Easy for him to say. I don't know how it can.

Shaan says, "Abby, we can't walk over and see each other tomorrow. We'll both be on planes, heading home. When will we meet again?"

I want to yell out and tell the world how unfair all this is.

Shaan's look says *I can't bear this either. We at least need a kiss.* Okay, maybe I'm reading into his look a little too much. But a first kiss and a good-bye kiss in one? Too tragic.

Shiva might have somehow tuned into my wicked thoughts. He decides that the monstrous rubber plant in the corner needs some love. He begins to dust and shine each leaf with a damp cloth. Seriously.

I think I might sneak Shaan to my room and walk toward the staircase but Grandma Tara reminds me that we entertain guests in the living room, before she goes to her own room to rest.

Shaan and I return to the living room, and Shaan unfolds a map from his pocket. He traces the distance between Houston and Dallas. I trace along, so our fingers could touch.

As a last ditch attempt I ask Shiva for a Coke for Shaan.

Shiva gives me an angelic smile and asks Bina to get a one and he continues to swipe the next rubber leaf.

Can a person feel hostility toward a leaf?

With Shiva as a guardian, dragons and moats would be unnecessary.

From the kitchen there is the loudest clanging of pots plunging to the floor. Shiva swears and runs to look.

I jump up to rush after Shiva, but Shaan holds my wrist firm. He pulls me behind the gleaming rubber plant. We look at each other. Our bodies are close, and just like that, he kisses me. Blink of an eye. The pressure of firm but soft Shaan lips.

There's no mistaking it; this is my first official kiss.

Shiva is back.

We quickly part.

Shiva looks at us suspiciously and swears at Bina's clumsiness.

Salima arrives to help Grandma Tara and me get ready for the premiere. "Abby, there will be photographers wanting to get a shot of you after all those headlines."

The red carpet is at five o'clock, followed by the movie screening. The after-party is at nine. Shiva says it will go on until dawn. My flight leaves at two, but I have to get to the airport much earlier.

Shaan and I hug. It's time for good-byes.

"Go get 'em, Abby!"

After he leaves, I notice a handmade card on the table with my name on it. It's a picture of us outside the Mandir Cinema with Dad's huge poster in the background.

It reads, *Abby, I still have to teach you to play cricket, and your Hindi seriously stinks. So let's meet soon. Will miss you until then. Shaan.*

I read it a few more times and clutch it close. I wish I don't have to go to the premiere so I can retreat to my room and relive all my moments with Shaan.

I wish I had his confidence. I knew I would physically live through this mess, but would my relationship with Dad survive?

❧ CHAPTER 26 ❧
RED CARPET, WHITE LIES

Dad gestures at the newspapers. "Despite this mess the show must go on!"

Grandma Tara nods in agreement.

Salima supervises Dad's hair and makeup staff as they get Grandma Tara and me ready. The makeup woman gushes over my "young, innocent" skin until I blush. She shampoos and styles my hair. Then she does my makeup. At the end, each one of my features pops. The makeup is so subtle it's barely there. It's magic! Finally, I slip on my dress, sandals, and Grandma Tara's earrings. Another one of the moments I will remember forever. At each stage, I ask Salima to take pictures so I can share them with Mom and my friends at home.

I feel like Princess Abby descending the stairs. Grandma Tara is speechless. She extends both her arms and gives me a hug. Then she mutters something about warding off the evil eye.

Dad looks beyond handsome in a suit. "Great dress, Abby!" he says and I beam. Just for a minute, he seems less distant. He's been quiet and preoccupied since this morning's headlines.

I sit in the back of the car, sandwiched between Dad and Grandma Tara. Thomas sits up front and Shiva drives as usual. We're on our way to the red carpet premiere.

I'm beyond nervous—I'm petrified. Everyone is quiet in the car, gearing up for the craziness. I can tell Dad is tense from the way he drums his fingers on his thigh.

When I chose the cream-colored dress with the poppies bursting at the hemline, I'd imagined the premiere being a walk in the park. I'd be a spectator but with the perks of being an insider. So much for that.

Unfortunately, now I'm the focus of attention. Dad called the newspaper headlines lurid. I looked it up, and apparently loud, sensational attention was certainly coming my way.

Thomas turns and says, "Even negative publicity is still publicity. Let's pray it doesn't hurt the film."

Dad gives Thomas a cold, furious look. If I were Thomas, I would have visibly shriveled up. I never want to be at the receiving end of that look from Dad. My string quartet plays a horror film sound track.

Grandma Tara shakes her head and tsks.

Shiva stops at the next traffic light. "No traffic at the Haji Ali junction, we reach in fifteen minutes."

"Call the theater staff, Thomas. Let them know," says Dad.

Grandma Tara adjusts her sari again, even though it looks perfect.

My hand feels disconnected from my brain as I mechanically brush my hair. I touch Grandma's earrings.

"At last. My own home production," says Dad as the car inches to a stop.

Throngs of fans are cordoned off from the red carpet by the police. I've never seen so many people screaming except on TV and the reality is as different as seeing the Niagara Falls in a picture and hearing it gush and roar in front of you. The frantic energy of the crowd startles me. They lean against the barricades, straining to touch Dad, his car, even his shadow. People are perched on top of trees and buildings to get a glimpse of him. I shrink into the seat.

Dad rolls down the window and waves. A fresh swell of shrieks. Naveen! Naveen!

He opens the door and steps onto the red carpet. I hear a barrage of clicks. He leans in and gives me his arm. For an instant I can't move. Is ducking behind the seat and telling Shiva to drive me away as fast as he can to the airport an option?

"Abby," Dad's voice is warm.

Grandma Tara's hand presses the small of my back to urge me on.

I take Dad's hand and step onto the carpet. The cameras explode. The flashing lights blind and I fight the urge to shield my eyes. If it weren't for Dad's arm, I would've buckled. The spotlight feels like a harsh naked bulb that swings and blinds during police interrogations in movies.

"Smile, Abby," Dad reminds me like a ventriloquist without letting his lips move.

He holds on to me as he helps Grandma Tara out of the car. The three of us cross the red carpet together. It's only a few feet but it feels longer than the track at school on a hundred-degree Texas summer day.

"Naveen, introduce us to your daughter!"

"Why have you been hiding her?"

"Where is her mother?"

"Do you have other children we don't know about?"

Jeez! Are you kidding me? Do you think he has kids strewn around?

I want to snap back but I know better now, and I can feel Dad's hand tightening on my arm, reminding me to keep them from get under my skin.

"Abby! Abby!"

Dad does not respond to any of these questions.

No one asks a single question about his film—just as he feared. So much for Dad wanting the focus to be on his film and his work rather than on his personal life.

My heart sinks. I want to scream at these morons.

Blinding camera lights continue to flash. Dad smiles and so does Grandma Tara. I change my deer in the headlights look to a phony smile.

Then I see two girls around my age carrying a homemade poster as high as their arms would allow.

We heart Abby! Welcome to India.

I want to thank them. *They* don't care how long I've been in Dad's life.

Then one reporter out of the hordes yells out, "Naveen, your new film is different. Tell us why you made it."

I wanted to hug the one sane man among the crazies.

Dad pauses. "It is different. I produced the film I always wanted to make and I hope you all like it. I'm proud of it. I would love to talk to you after you've seen the movie," he says and shakes the reporter's hand.

Seizing the chance, someone asks, "Has Rani met Abby?"

Dad turns away, his jaw clenched. Almost at the end of the red carpet, we hear yells. "Rani's here!" echoes the crowd, and the frenzy takes over one more time. The cameras turn on her. Dad continues to talk to the one reporter. I watch Rani.

Rani is at her glamorous best with flawless makeup and hair. Nothing like the dressed-down Rani who I shared ice cream with. Today she is Rani, the screen goddess. Her peacock-blue silk sari is like a second skin. How can you wear six yards of fabric and still show so much skin? I should do a research paper on that topic. Anyway, she manages to wear a sari and make it look like she needs more clothes. Maybe a sweatshirt to cover her up. Ha!

She's the focus of all the attention. She glides along the carpet, answers questions with a giggle, and greets Dad coyly. I watch her and the hundreds of scrambling reporters. Then someone asks her about me and I freeze. The practiced professional, Rani smiles and says, "Abby and I love spending time together."

Other celebrities arrive. Each time there's a wave of recognition and shrieks. OMG. I just absorb it all and feel giddy.

A sea of people greets us inside the theater too. There are other members of the cast and crew and they all want to meet Naveen Kumar's daughter.

Rani takes me aside. "Abby, are you okay?" she whispers, referring of course to the leaking of the story.

My eyes shimmer in response.

"Naveen told me about the photographer. I'm sorry." She squeezes my hand.

Then someone whisks Rani away. Cast and crew continue to mingle. I smile for picture after picture with Dad and countless others until my mouth hurt. Salima comes and finally leads Grandma Tara and me to our seats.

Then the lights dim. The movie starts and the audience of invited guests enthusiastically claps and whistles.

I should have asked Dad to invite Shaan. Was he thinking of me? I wish he were here whispering in my ear. That's a reason to not learn Hindi. Shaan could translate for me forever.

The possibility of not seeing Shaan again makes me sick to my stomach. Why do I have to meet the perfect boy only to have him live in a different city?

I miss Mom. Is she making coffee? Is she scrambling to get to the café on time? Is she baking my favorite apple pie to welcome me home? What will she think of all this?

The movie has romance and musical numbers like Dad's previous movies, but it has a grittier plot and more of Dad in it—his words and his feelings. He plays the idealistic investigative reporter. I can hear him in the dialogue. I recognize one of the pictures in our house used in the movie. I spot Shiva in one of the street scenes.

I'm an insider.

He's the everyman hero fighting corruption and bad guys like the publicity blurbs said.

I've read all the press articles about him and I understand what they meant about how Dad dominates the screen. I now know that the opening box office could make or break a movie. Then I come prancing in and take the focus away from his film.

The credits roll, and the audience claps, hugs, and thump one another on the back. Admirers mob Dad and Rani. Grandma and I clap until our hands are sore.

Grandma Tara beams as she watches Dad accepting all the congratulations from his fans. I squeeze her hand. I knew how she feels because I'm proud of him too.

Salima drives us to the after party in a nearby five-star hotel with polished floors, fabulous Indian art, and views of the city lights.

Posters of the movie stare at us from the walls. CDs of the movie sound track for Dad and Rani to sign for the guests are piled high on tables. Perfumed women in diamonds and chiffon and silk saris air kisses. Music from the film plays over the speakers. Tables groan under samosas, chicken tikka, *pakoras*, Chinese dumplings, vegetarian sushi, pastries, and *gulab jamun*.

I know in a few hours I'll be at the airport, boarding my flight home and I can't eat a bite. Especially not after how sick I got on the flight here! I stare at the vegetable sculptures that decorate the platters and fight back regrets.

"Abby, I am tired," says Grandma Tara. "Do you mind if we skip the party and go home and be together?"

I almost hug her in relief. This is the first time she's gone out except for doctor visits since she was ill. Of course she's tired. And so am I.

From the corner of my eye, I can see Dad and Rani approach us.

"You say your good-byes, I'll wait for you." Grandma Tara takes a seat on a sofa nearby.

Can we make a dash for it? The thought of saying good-bye to Dad and Rani makes me choke up. I can't think of anything I want to do less.

Rani hugs me with surprising warmth. "Abby. I know you're leaving in a few hours. I'm so sorry we couldn't spend more time together. You look beautiful. This dress is so you."

She kisses my cheek and I hug her.

"I'll leave you and your dad to say your good-byes."

Dad looks sheepish. He holds my shoulders. "I hate good-byes, Abby. It's not my thing."

Another thing we have in common, Dad, I want to say. I gulp.

"Your grandmother wants to take you home. You have a little more than an hour before you have to leave for the airport," he says looking at his wristwatch.

Then he looks into my eyes. "Abby, I wish things could

have been different, and you could have stayed longer, but I know you have to leave today to make it back to school. Thank you for coming. You have no idea how much it meant to your grandmother."

Before he can say more or I can tell him I love him, a bunch of noisy people walk over and ask to meet me. They seem to be Dad's childhood friends. Dad introduces me as his daughter.

I don't register anyone's names.

More chitter chatter.

Grandma Tara reminds us it's time to go. Dad hugs me again, and then Grandma Tara, Salima, and I are in the car, and Shiva was driving us home. I guess that's fine, neither of us likes good-byes anyway.

In the car, I replay Dad's words. I know how much my visit meant to Grandma Tara already. But what had it meant to him?

He said he wished it had been different. How?

Does he wish I hadn't ruined it all?

Did he really mean that he wishes I could stay longer? I know what a great actor he is already. Was he acting?

I stare at the lights twinkling around Marine Drive and remember when Dad told me that they're called the Queen's Necklace. Through the moisture in my eyes, the lights flare and melt.

☙ CHAPTER 27 ❧
ARRIVALS AND DEPARTURES

I take off Grandma's earrings in my room and place them back in their little velvet box. I can't possibly take them, not after what I did. I snap the box shut with regret and leave a note on the dresser saying, *Grandma Tara, I'm sorry. I don't deserve to have them. Abby.*

While saying good-bye, Grandma Tara hugs me a million times. She obviously does not dislike good-byes. She holds my face between her soft, lined hands and says, "*Beta*, I want to get strong again so I can travel to America and see you graduate. Thank you for coming to see me."

What can I say to that? You're welcome? My words are stuck in my throat.

She smiles at me and says, "At my age you can't leave

unfinished business. Abby, I do wish life had been different. Naveen and I will go through all of my husband's papers. We should have done it years ago."

The lump in my throat is a boulder. I nod.

I will not bawl.

My knees feel weak as I walk out the door.

I want to say *I'll see you soon*, but don't trust myself to speak.

Do people miss trouble? No one, not even Grandma Tara, had invited me back.

After looking back at her one last time, I get into the car, and Shiva drives me to the airport. I check my watch, a few minutes before midnight.

I look out into the night. What if Dad's film flops? I shake my head as if it's an Etch-A-Sketch and I can wipe the thoughts away. Unfortunately, it doesn't work that way.

At the airport, a chaperone meets us in the lobby.

"Abby, I remember you!" Shiva's voice is weighed with emotion.

"Oh, Shiva, I will think of you too!" I say.

He extends his hand. Maybe he thinks it might be inappropriate to do anything else or maybe he's embarrassed. I don't care. I hug him tight. Startled and thoroughly uncomfortable, he pats my back.

I leave before I get too emotional.

My chaperone whisks me through immigration, customs, and security. It's all a big blur.

When called to board, I turn and walk around the waiting area again. As if I need to see India with all its contrasts and beauty and its warm people one last time.

"Are you okay?" the flight attendant asks when she sees my dejected face.

"I'm fine," I reply.

She gives me an uncertain smile and walks down the aisle. A few minutes later, she returns with a questioning smile and a sealed blanket, "Aren't you Naveen Kumar's daughter?" she asks. "I thought I saw you in the newspaper."

I wrinkle my nose. "I am. I hope the headlines you read weren't too nasty."

The flight attendant blushes.

Now there's a difference from ten days ago. I can admit to being my father's daughter publicly.

Buckling up, I think back to when I had yearned to meet my father. Now I know my father, my grandmother, Shiva, Mina, Bina, Rani, Salima, and so many others.

When the plane takes off, I'm exhausted from feeling so much. I had my first kiss but the boy I like lives in a different city. I should be glad he lives in the same state, I know, but why can't he be in my city? Not fair!

When will I see Dad again? Ever?

There are so many things I wanted to see and do. I wanted to see the Taj Mahal and the Rajasthan Desert with Dad and attend a cricket match and learn Hindi, eat Shiva's paneer, and attend a big fat Indian wedding, and get henna done on my hands.

Will we exchange Christmas and birthday cards? Even my orthodontist sends me those.

The thought of Dad communicating as often as the orthodontist is the last straw. The tears come in bursts like the dancing sprinkler at the water park.

The woman sitting next to me looks alarmed. On my way over, I scared away my co-passenger by barfing. Now I'm hysterically sobbing.

And when I sob, I snort and set off my sinuses. So then I have to blow my nose. Honk! Honk!

There's a goose in first class. Awesome.

Abby, seriously, get a grip, or the airlines will put you on a no fly list.

Twenty-eight exhausting hours later, Mom stands outside the customs gate with her arms outstretched. "Abby!" she shrieks. "Abby!"

I ran the last few feet. Not easy to do while pushing a cart loaded with suitcases. I get a look and an under-her-breath "Kids these days!" from a woman wearing pearls and a boxy suit.

Mom and I hug.

"It's good to be back, Mom."

Mom holds me at arm's length and looks me over. Then she hugs me again. "Oh Abby, I missed you."

At last, I'm with someone whose life I haven't messed up.

The air is crisp and cool when we step out.

The drive home makes me aware of how much I've taken for granted. The wide, clean roads, the relatively cleaner air, the uncontaminated water, and Mom.

We drive straight to Grandma and Grandpa's house.

Grandma has saved leftovers from Thanksgiving for dinner. Grandpa does what he calls a jig, singing, "Happy, happy, Thanksgiving, dear Sparkles!" and swings me around the kitchen.

I've missed Grandpa calling me Sparkles. In spite of my fatigue and jetlag, I make a plate, loading it with turkey, stuffing, and mashed potatoes, and of course pie.

I'm home.

I feel a twinge when I look at my wristwatch, still on India time.

Before I eat, I dial Dad's phone number to let them know I reached home.

Shiva answers. "A-bby," he says. "A-bby, you in home."

"Yes, Shiva, I am." Thousands of miles away.

"I make *pooris*, but you not here," he says.

"Oh, eat one for me," I reply.

Then in turns, I speak to Grandma Tara and even Mina and Bina.

Dad isn't home.

Grandma Tara says he's in Delhi for the premiere and will be doing a whirlwind publicity tour, visiting a different city each day for the next ten days.

"Abby, this morning I woke up and you weren't practicing your violin. I miss your music. Record songs and mail them," says Grandma Tara. "Naveen called and said to tell you he misses you and will talk to you once he's home."

Why can't he call me himself? Is Grandma Tara making up the part about Dad saying he misses me? Maybe he's forgotten me already and Grandma Tara is being kind.

"The house is not the same without you, Abby," Grandma Tara says before she hangs up.

I miss them all already.

I want a *poori* on my Thanksgiving plate. I want to clone myself and be in two places.

I show Mom, Grandma, and Grandpa some of the million pictures I took.

Before falling asleep, I call Priya and tell her about the newspapers and how the story was leaked, but ever-optimistic Priya wants to talk about the premiere and how she saw me on Asian satellite TV instead.

"Abby, I recorded the red carpet, and I loved your dress.

I'll host a viewing party. You'll be the guest of honor of course. Vivian, Karishma, Emma, Michelle, and Zoey are coming. Did I forget anyone? I'll buy some red construction paper and make a red carpet. Should I tell my Mom to fry some samosas?"

Priya is on a roll. She doesn't really need me to say or suggest anything.

At least I still have my friends.

I decide to text Shaan. *Hey. It's Abby. I'm home.*

Almost instantly my phone pings. He's been waiting for me to get home. Smug happy dance.

Can you walk over? Sigh ☺

I text back. *I would if I could.* Too bold?

I would if I could too, Abby. ☺ *Can I call you? I want to hear your voice.*

Of course you can ☺

I want to hear his voice too. I also want to grin back at his silly goofy smile.

I answer the phone on the first ring. His familiar voice makes me miss him more.

"It feels weird," I tell him. "Like I'm not sure where I am. After being on the plane so long I feel like I can still hear the drone when I close my eyes, and one of my ears hasn't popped either."

"How was the premiere? Your dad?"

"It was all awful. The stupid press kept asking him about me instead of his movie. One of them even asked Dad if he had more hidden kids."

"You're kidding," Shaan interrupts. "Like he has kids hidden in his attic?"

"Exactly. His movie was great though. Way more interesting than me. Why don't they get it? Knuckleheads."

"Abby, I miss you already."

"I miss you too, Shaan," I say.

I brushed my hair smiling after we finish our call. My head hits the pillow but my eyes fly open.

I'm an idiot. How does all this matter? Yes, I'd been quite the hit with Grandma Tara, Shiva, Mina, Bina, and Shaan, but...

I screwed up the one relationship I went to Mumbai to find.

Dad hates me.

He doesn't even want to talk to me.

He didn't come to the airport to see me off.

He didn't want to talk to me on my last day in Mumbai.

He smiled and looked normal on the red carpet and at the party because he's the best actor in the world and there were fans around us the whole time.

I open my violin case to check it and my eyes bulge.

Every single string had popped.

My sane mind says strings often pop due to cabin

pressure changes on airplanes. However, a louder part of me says maybe it's an omen.

Broken strings = broken relationship.

☙ CHAPTER 28 ☙
SPECIAL DELIVERY

For the first few days home, I live in a weird world. I have to remind myself of where I am and who with. I have two families in two countries and two different cultures. Weirdville. Jet lag dogs me and I wake up at three in the morning and relive the mistakes I made. I can't forget or forgive myself.

Shaan texts me a lot and I text him back. I have to tell him that I don't have unlimited texting and Mom will kill me when she sees the bill. He says his Mom would too. So we Facebooked instead.

In Mumbai, people drive on the left side of the road. The first morning home, I thought Mom made a turn onto the wrong side of the street and cried out, "Watch it!"

Startled the heck out of her.

That week I jumped each time the phone rang. Was it

Dad? No, it was a marketing call selling us new siding or a vacation to Bermuda.

It's been a week and he hasn't called. I stop hoping and feel hollowed out like a rotting Halloween pumpkin without the candle glowing in it.

The next week in Algebra as I plough through my equation, the intercom crackles and interrupts. "Could you please send Abby Spencer to the office?"

Huh? Why? Which rule did I break?

I walk the long corridor to the office filled with dread even though I can't think of any crime I've committed against Roosevelt Middle School.

It turns out I missed a few things on my enrollment form at the beginning of the school year. The office missed it too and forwarded them to wherever forms go. All these months later, someone realized and sent the form back to the school. Whew!

It asks for real basic information and Mom already signed it so the office person says, "Take a few minutes and fill it out right now."

"Sure," I say, taking the clipboard, pen, and form.

I filled out name, address, phone number, you know, the standard lalalalala. Then I stop in my laced-up boots.

Race (Optional): Caucasian, African American, Hispanic, Asian, Pacific Islander, Other. With a blank that you can fill out.

I've checked Caucasian all these years, even though I knew my father is Indian. His absence made me want to snub him. Now it's different. My identity is a combination of two cultures.

I stare at the blank hypnotized. Two phones ring together and strangely remind me of my days in Mumbai when Dad's phones would ring simultaneously in the house.

Deliberately, I write *biracial.*

I smile with satisfaction when I'm done. As if I've done something important. Even if Dad doesn't care enough to call me.

For the first time in my life, I fill in my father's name, address, and phone number. Because I can. Even if the school is unlikely to contact him in case of emergencies in Mumbai!

I hand the form to the woman at the desk and walk back to class with a skip in my step. I may not have much of a relationship with my father but it's better than never having met him.

That evening, Mom is working late. The holidays are a busy time of year for her. I have the house to myself and I decide to wrap some Christmas presents.

I gather the scissors, tape, and gifts I'd bought for my grandparents and Mom in Mumbai. I wrap the kurta I bought for Grandpa with Dad's help. For Grandma Spencer, I bought some pure cotton paisley place mats. Grandma loves setting creative tables and I know she'll love these.

I bought a small box for Mom to match her memory box. I place a picture of me and Dad inside. I also bought her a scarf in a riot of colors. I can see her wearing it with her little black dress.

As I stick a bow on the last package I think that Dad is probably at the end of his publicity blitz tour by now. I texted once but didn't hear back. Why can't he take a moment to text me back?

My stomach rumbles. Dinnertime.

Mom left some pasta for me but I'm in the mood for a grilled cheese, crispy on the outside and melty, gooey on the inside. I wander to the refrigerator to grab some cheese, bread, and butter, and stack them all in my hands like Rachael Ray, and put the pan on.

The doorbell rings as I'm about to slide the bread into the melting butter. I turn off the stove and go to the door.

I'm not allowed to open the door when I'm alone at home unless it's my grandparents or my neighbor.

I peek through the frosted glass. A man stands, hunched with his hands in his pockets. I can see his back as he faces our front yard. My heartbeat gallops and then stops. No way!

Am I hallucinating? Could it be?

That back and those shoulders, I would know them anywhere. It can't be! Or can it?

Rules be darned, I throw the door open.

He turns around. "Home delivery!" he says and holds out a familiar box of earrings. He grins from ear to ear.

I have goose bumps all over. Does Mom know about this? Did she keep it a secret?

Dad?

He laughs at my shocked face.

"You forgot your earrings. Your Grandma wanted me to deliver them to you. I also have a special magazine for you."

I step out and fling myself in his arms. He almost falls over but steadies himself and hugs me tight. I can barely breathe.

"Dad, you're in Houston. What? How?" I blabber, completely shocked.

Then we both look at each other and laugh.

Dad was standing there in the flesh outside my house.

"Are you going to invite me in? It's a bit cold out here," Dad says, laughing.

"Of course," I say, dragging him in. I clutch the box and the magazine tight.

Dad looks around our decorated house and says, "I love being in America at Christmas. I imagined Meredith's house being like this. Homey."

He walks to the tree and hones in on an ornament with a picture of a gap-toothed me.

"Abby, can I get some coffee? I need to stay awake for a few more hours, but my eyes want to close this minute."

"Of course," I say.

He washes up.

I'm brewing coffee for Dad in my house in Houston. Is this real? I pinch myself. Can I even make coffee worth drinking? I mimic what I've seen Mom do.

I quickly pick up the wrapping paper and stuff off the table to tidy up the kitchen.

I imitate Mom again and light the candle sitting on the table.

Then very deliberately, I slip on *my* heirloom earrings. The string quartet bows furiously. I'm so happy it trips all over itself.

Dad sniffs when he comes back to the kitchen. "Abby, I like the gingerbread perfume."

He likes our house and our candle. I feel all warm.

"I'll tell Grandma Tara you wore your earrings as soon as you could."

Then we're quiet. The silence suddenly challenges us. I don't know what to say, where to begin. Luckily, Dad takes the lead.

"Abby, sit down. We need to talk. I've been thinking about what happened during the last days of your trip to India." He weaves his hands through his hair. "I have so much to learn about being a father, a parent."

"I ruined it all," I interrupt.

"No," he says, placing his hand on mine. "No, you didn't, Abby. I didn't think that for a moment. I was angry at the press, worried about my movie. I shut down and don't talk when I'm that furious and upset. Rani helped me see that. It worked for me before, when I was married to my career."

"Oh, Dad, I did my part too," I say.

"Abby, you're the kid. As an adult, it took me a while to learn to deal with the photographers. I'm supposed to be the parent, the adult. I should have comforted you, made sure you knew that I was not angry with you, but frustrated at the situation. In my defense, I have not been a parent for long. Will you give your old dad a second chance?"

"Yes, yes, yes!" I yell. My face will split from my grin. I dance. A happy, joyful, ungainly dance.

Dad looks touched. "I have so much time to make up for and it will take me a while but I'm determined to get it right."

We look at each other, happy.

His forehead scrunched, he says, "There's more. Abby, your Grandma Tara and I went through all of my father's papers and we found the letter that Meredith sent me all those years ago. My father did not open it or give it to me. Your Grandma Tara thinks that he was afraid I would return to America and he didn't want to lose his son. He didn't know that your mom was pregnant. I am so sorry. I honestly don't know how life would have been for all of us if he had read that letter."

So much to take in. I don't know how to feel.

"I'm sorry," Dad whispers. "I feel so helpless."

We hug and are silent for a while.

"Dad…" I hesitate. Do I really want to know? "Did the press stop the ugly stuff?"

"Yesterday's newspapers line today's garbage cans. They'll get over it," he said. "I realized that my fans were more loyal than I gave them credit for."

Whew! I haven't ruined Dad's career.

Then I have to ask. "Dad, why didn't you call or answer my text after I left Mumbai?"

"I wanted to surprise you in person. I discussed it with your mom and she played along. I toured the major Indian cities and then took two days to get here. Abby, I have three days before I report for my next movie, which is shooting in Toronto. I want to spend that time with you. Get to know your school, your friends, your city."

I whoop for joy. "You can come to Priya's viewing party tonight. She will die!"

He picks up the magazine that we've both forgotten in our excitement. It's the issue of *Film World* with our photo shoot.

"I think it turned out well. Don't you?" He hands it to me. We're on the cover! In the photo, Dad sits on a bench and I stand behind him, my hands on his shoulders. I think back to the day that the news leaked in Mumbai. The editor of *Film World* had called. Disappointed that she did not have the scoop anymore, Maya recovered fast. She was still the first one to have real posed pictures and an interview with us. All the headlines would only make fans more eager to read and see more. She'd put us on the cover and she'd print more copies of the issue.

We look amazing.

I open the double spread. These two really like each other, I think as I stare at the picture of Dad and me goofing around.

I sniff. So does Dad. I wonder what's burning. I look back at the picture. The smell is stronger, harder to ignore.

We're on fire! Literally.

I jump to my feet.

"Abby, the magazine is on fire. It was too close to the candle," Dad says as he grabs the magazine from my hand and runs to the sink and turns the faucet on.

The last thing I need is to burn down the house. I run to the closest bathroom and fill a pitcher of water. I throw it at the magazine and Dad. The flames were already out. Now Dad is drenched too.

Wouldn't you know it? Then the smoke alarm goes off. Shrill, loud, and obnoxious. I run and open the windows to let the smoke out of the kitchen. It doesn't help.

The alarm continues to buzz.

I'm scared the entire neighborhood and the world will know by now. Our neighbor hears the alarm, knows I'm usually alone at this time of evening, and calls Mom and my grandparents.

Within minutes, they're all at the house. We've managed to make the fire alarm stop shrieking by then. Dad and I assure them that all is fine.

Mom and Dad are hesitant, unsure as they meet each other. "Meredith," he says, "It's been a long time."

"Yes," she replies, her face red, smoothing her skirt. "Yes, it has."

"You look the same as you did fourteen years ago," he says.

Then they do this weird kind of handshake turned hug.

Could they get back together? Maybe if we were in a Bollywood movie, but this is real life. And there is Rani too.

"Meredith, I have to thank you for raising Abby alone. We have so much to talk about."

They have a lot of catching up to do.

If I had any doubts about Dad's ability to win over people, they are gone after I see him with my grandparents.

"This sauce is the best I have ever eaten," he says to Grandma as he reaches for a second helping of her spaghetti and meatballs.

He admires Grandpa's handiwork around the house and asks, "When are you two coming to visit me in Mumbai?"

"Well now," says Grandpa pleased, "we'll have to plan that, won't we?"

That night, Priya greets me at her door with "Abby Spencer, you are late!"

I can barely keep the grin from my face. Her party's guest list has grown. I can see at least ten girls behind her.

I take a deep breath. "Well, since you rolled out a red carpet," I say, pointing to the construction paper, "I thought I'd bring along a real, live movie star."

On cue, Dad gets out of the car and saunters up to the door.

The girls inside shriek in disbelief.

Priya is speechless.

Her mom makes some garbled sounds and then faints. Luckily, she's quick to revive and we don't need to call 911.

After things calm down, I show them the magazine cover. Even though one copy is a charred mess, Dad has a few more copies in his suitcase. Lots of oohs and aahs!

Dad asks them if I've told them about Shaan and me being in a song in his next film. Priya and Zoey's faces are priceless.

"Dad," I say. "I didn't tell them because I didn't think we'd make it in the movie. We could be cut, you know."

Dad grins. "I do have some influence. I plan to make sure that you kids stay."

More shrieks. Then it's performance time.

Dad takes out his iPod as planned and plays the song from the movie and I play it on my violin, which I'd bought along.

Dad and I teach them the *dhak, dhak, dhin* moves. Shake, shake, twirl, and bump. Dancing + happy = happy dancing late into the night.

I'll never forget that party. Ever.

I text Shaan and fill him in. If only he could be there, it would be complete.

The next morning, Dad insists on coming to Mom's store. We tie on our aprons and get to work.

Mrs. Harris, one of Mom's regulars, looks over at Dad, and winks at me as she leaves with her chocolate chiffon pie. "My, my!"

"He's my dad," I say, and she turns bright red.

I text Priya that Dad is at the store. She tells her mom who beats the drums and makes sure the entire community knows. Every South Asian person in Houston must have come to buy a pie that morning.

Mom has to call in the reserves—Grandma and Grandpa!

With a pie in my hand, I look around me. I have to literally stop and take in the moment and capture it and savor it like a bite of blueberry pie.

Dad is at the counter, Grandma running the cash register. Grandpa coaxes the crowd into order and Mom runs back and forth replenishing pies. All the people I love, my entire family, are with me, around me, and my heart feels as light as a balloon floating above a field of bluebonnets. If only Grandma Tara were here! But I know I'll see her again.

"Hey, Dad," I say, looking at the empty pastry case at noon, "you didn't tell me how your movie did."

"It wasn't important, Abby." But then he beams. "It smashed all box office records. I plan to start a charitable foundation in Mumbai with some of the profits. "Will you come down and help me?"

"I'll be there to help you when summer rolls around," I promise.

They are the best three days. There is a once-in-a-decade dusting of snow in Houston. Only appropriate. Dad is here. It's a miracle. Even the weather gods understand that.

I'm so content I almost don't need presents for Christmas. Almost. The string quartet merrily plays "Rudolph the Red-Nosed Reindeer."

"He's my dad," I say. "Meet my dad." I say it a million times during those days, and—believe me—it never gets old.

ACKNOWLEDGMENTS

Kelly Barrales-Saylor at Albert Whitman edited this book and made it stronger. Kristin Zelazko has an amazing eye for detail and made sure Abby's journey was on schedule.

My agent Jill Corcoran's enthusiastic response to this story carried Abby and me through the journey.

Gratitude goes to Cynthia Leitich Smith and Kathi Appelt, who helped me believe that I could write. They have hearts as big as Texas.

Thank you to my readers and writing friends: Vonna, Kathy, Marty, Laura, Russell, Melissa, Shelli, Vicki, Liz, Chris, and Joy.

My biggest thanks go to my family. Karishma wanted me to write a "happy story about India."

Samir's zest for life is reflected in my writing. Rajeev's quiet strength is my anchor.

Thank you to my Dad, Shashi Walavalkar, who read every line of the manuscript and has been present every day of my life.

 **VARSHA BAJAJ** was born and raised in Mumbai, home to the Indian film industry. Some of the characters she saw growing up had to find a place in her novel!

She came to America in 1986, and now lives in Houston with her husband, kids, and adorable dog.